"Marry me, Stevie."

What did he just say?

"We can give this child the type of home and family you and I both wanted," he said. "You'll get the help you need, and I'll get to be a dad."

She always acted on impulse, followed her hunches. Every one of those usual prompts urged her now to accept Cole's offer.

It wasn't the hearts-and-flowers-and-violins proposal she'd imagined, but she was a mother now. And if she was honest, Cole ticked every item on the list of attributes she'd want for her child's father. He was stable, dependable, practical. So...

"Yes."

He went still. "Yes?"

"Yes," she repeated.

"Great! We'll make this work, Stevie. I promise." He turned to go, then stopped.

"That was a lousy way to conclude a proposal, wasn't it?" he asked. "I can do better." Then he gathered her into his arms and gave her a kiss.

How could she have known the quiet analyst next door kissed like a dashing pirate?

And that she was nearly leveled by, of all men, her neighbor, friend...and soon-to-be convenient husband?

* * *

PROPOSALS & PROMISES:
Putting a ring on it is only the beginning!

Dear Reader

I grew up surrounded by a big Southern family: my parents, three brothers, grandparents, aunts, uncles and too many cousins to count. As my brothers and I married and started families of our own, holiday gatherings became larger and noisier. We had plenty of food, laughter, gossip and chatter—and children. Always children. Some related by blood, others through marriage or adoption, but all welcomed with open arms. My parents were "Nana and Papa" to all—even kids just visiting for an afternoon—and there was always love enough for more. We lost my mom a few years ago, but her legacy lives on in the hearts and memories of all the children she spoiled with hugs and home-baked cookies.

In *The Bachelor's Little Bonus*, hardworking professionals Stephanie "Stevie" McLane and Cole McKellar are ready to create their own families, though neither expects the circumstances that will bring them together. It begins as a marriage of convenience for the sake of Stevie's unborn child, but it doesn't take long before they realize that what they both want is a real marriage, a family united by lifelong commitment.

I hope you enjoy the journey these two independent skeptics take as they learn that romance can last a lifetime and that family is not defined by blood, but by love.

Happy reading!

Gina Wilkins

The Bachelor's Little Bonus

Gina Wilkins

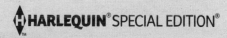
HARLEQUIN® SPECIAL EDITION®

Recycling programs
for this product may
not exist in your area

ISBN-13: 978-0-373-65960-9

The Bachelor's Little Bonus

Copyright © 2016 by Gina Wilkins

This edition published by arrangement with Harlequin Books S.A.

For questions and comments about the quality of this book,
please contact us at CustomerService@Harlequin.com.

Printed in U.S.A.

Author of more than one hundred titles for Harlequin, native Arkansan **Gina Wilkins** was introduced early to romance novels by her avid-reader mother. Gina loves sharing her own stories with readers who enjoy books celebrating families and romance. She is inspired daily by her husband of over thirty years, their two daughters and their son, their librarian son-in-law who fit perfectly into this fiction-loving family, and an adorable grandson who already loves books.

Books by Gina Wilkins

Harlequin Special Edition

Proposals & Promises

The Boss's Marriage Plan
A Reunion and a Ring

Bride Mountain

Healed with a Kiss
A Proposal at the Wedding
Matched by Moonlight

A Match for the Single Dad
The Texan's Surprise Baby
The Right Twin
His Best Friend's Wife
Husband for a Weekend

Doctors in the Family

Doctors in the Wedding
A Home for the M.D.
The M.D. Next Door

Visit the Author Profile page
at Harlequin.com for more titles.

For my family—
immediate, extended and family of the heart.
You have all enriched my life beyond measure.

Chapter One

Returning home from a mundane business trip, Cole McKellar stepped out of a dreary February evening and into a scene from one of his increasingly recurrent fantasies: A pretty blonde asleep on his oversized brown leather sofa.

The sight aroused and disturbed him—the same reaction he usually had to those unbidden daydreams. He squeezed his eyes shut, but when he opened them the blonde in question was still there. What was wrong with him? He shouldn't be having these feelings about Stevie, especially when she viewed him merely as a neighbor and a friend. And yet…

Illuminated by the lamp on the table nearest her head, she lay on her left side, her hand beneath her cheek, her jeans-covered legs drawn up in front of her. Her shoes were on the floor, leaving her feet exposed in bright red socks that matched her sweater. Golden curls tumbled around her sleep-flushed face, and her soft, full lips were slightly parted. Long lashes lay against her fair cheeks, hiding eyes he knew to be a vivid blue. Notably colorful and feminine in contrast to his muted bachelor decor, she looked young and vulnerable lying there, though he knew Stevie McLane to be a capable and accomplished thirty-one year old, only two years his junior.

Dusty, his little gray tabby, snuggled into the crook of Stevie's arm. In response to Cole's arrival, the cat lifted her head and gave him a look as though warning him not to disturb their sleeping guest. He frowned and studied Stevie more closely. Was there a trace of tears on her face? Had she been crying?

Gripping his overnight bag tightly in one hand, his computer case in the other, he shifted his weight uncomfortably, unsure what to do. Should he wake her? Should he let her sleep? He couldn't just stand here watching her. It was sort of…creepy.

Dusty stood and stretched. Roused by the movement, Stevie blinked her eyes open. Finding Cole standing there, she gasped.

The last thing he'd wanted to do was frighten her. "I'm sorry, Stevie, I—"

"Cole! I didn't—"

Both stopped talking to let the other speak, then hurried again to fill the awkward silence.

"I didn't mean to—"

"I thought you—"

Cole held up a hand with a rueful smile when their words overlapped again. "I'll start. I'm sorry I startled you. I didn't know you were here. Now your turn."

On her feet now, his next-door neighbor pushed back her tumbled hair with both hands and smiled up at him.

Though just over average height himself, he still felt as though he towered over Stevie, who topped out at about five-two in her red-stockinged feet. "I thought you weren't going to be home until tomorrow," she said.

"I rescheduled my flight because of the weather. I didn't want to get stuck in Dallas for an extra day or two, especially since I have to be in Chicago a few days next week."

"And now you must be tired." She shook her head. "I'm sorry, you weren't expecting to find uninvited company in your house."

She had no idea just what a welcome surprise that had been, nor would he fully enlighten her. When it came to Stevie, he'd gotten pretty good at concealing his feelings during the past year. "Usually when I come home, the house is empty except for Dusty, and she likes to play it cool with her royal greetings. It's a pleasant change to be welcomed with a smile."

He'd answered lightly while studying her suspiciously puffy eyelids. Would it be intrusive to mention his impression that she'd been crying? He settled for what he hoped was a vaguely concerned tone. "Is everything okay?"

She wiped nonchalantly at her cheeks, as if smoothing away the effects of sleep rather than any hint of tears. "Oh, sure. It was just too quiet at my house tonight, so Dusty and I were keeping each other company. I guess I fell asleep."

His cat had climbed on the arm of the couch and now demanded a greeting from him. Cole reached down to rub the tabby's soft, pointed ears. "Did you give Stevie your sad-eyes act to keep her from leaving after she fed you? I bet you added a few of those pitiful meows you've perfected."

Stevie wrinkled her nose with a little laugh. "I'm pretty sure she even threw in a couple of forlorn sniffles."

He ran a hand absently down Dusty's back, stopping to scratch at the base of the tail, a spot that always made his pet arch blissfully. "She's shameless."

"Yes, she is," Stevie agreed, giving the tabby a fond smile.

Cole claimed occasionally that he'd bought the cat with the house. He'd lived here only a couple weeks when a pathetic kitten had appeared on his doorstep out of a winter rainstorm, wet and hungry and miserable. Hearing the meows, he'd opened the door to investigate and the little stray had darted past him into the living room. Other than visits to the vet, she hadn't been outside since.

He'd planned initially to find a good home for the stray, but somehow she'd ended up staying. He and Dusty, who was named for her habit of emerging from under furniture with dust bunnies on her nose, got along like a couple of contented hermits. Still, it was always a treat for them when Stevie dropped by. Sometimes he thought they were both a little too eager for her visits.

Weren't cats and computer analysts supposed to be contentedly independent and naturally aloof? He'd wondered more than once what sort of special magic Stevie wielded to enchant them so thoroughly, though he hoped he was a bit more discreet about his fascination with her than his pet. He treasured his unconventional friendship with Stevie too much to risk it with the awkwardness of an unrequited infatuation.

A data analyst for a national medical group, Cole worked primarily from home. He made a few business trips a year for planning and progress meetings, but mostly he communicated with the outside world via computer and smartphone.

His late wife had teasingly accused him of taking introversion to the extreme. But it wasn't that he disliked people. He was just more comfortable with computers, especially since Natasha's difficult illness.

It was suddenly very quiet in the room. Pushing thoughts of the painful past from his mind, he cleared his throat and glanced toward the window. "Sounds like the sleet has stopped. Maybe it's finally changing over to snow. I'd rather have snow than ice."

Stevie nodded with a bit too much enthusiasm for the banal comments. "No kidding. At least this weather hit on a Friday so most people don't have to get out for work or school tomorrow. Not that local schools would be open, anyway. You know they close at the first sign of a snowflake. But still, I hope we get enough snow for the kids to build snowmen and have snowball fights. That's not something they get to do very often around here, so they'll want to make the most of it. I remember how disappointed I always was when we got all psyched up for snow and had to settle for just a dusting. Still, I hope it's gone by Monday. I have a couple of meetings I'd really hate to have to put off."

He chuckled, accustomed to her characteristic, stream-of-consciousness prattling. "Let's hope there's enough snow for the kids to enjoy over the weekend but that it melts quickly enough not to cause too many issues for the coming week."

"That would work." She smiled, but he had the distinct feeling something was wrong. For one thing, she was twisting a curl tightly around her fingertip, a nervous habit he'd noticed several times during the past few months.

Stevie was one of the most naturally effervescent women he'd ever known, outgoing and optimistic and a little quirky. She'd grown up in the comfortable bungalow on the corner lot next door in Little Rock, Arkansas. She'd been the first to welcome him to the street when he'd bought this house in the midtown neighborhood that was currently undergoing a revival after a decade-long slump. He'd made a tidy profit on the condo he'd sold last year, and he thought he'd do the same with this place if his needs changed again. Even better than that, he'd gained Stevie as a neighbor.

He wondered if it was only the bad weather that had left her free on a Friday night to keep his cat company and doze on his couch. As far as he knew, she hadn't dated anyone since a breakup some three months ago. When they'd first met, he'd had designs on her, and maybe he'd even had a few fantasies about her since, but he'd never acted on any of them. She'd been involved with the hipster musician, which had made her off-limits. Not that he had a chance with her anyway.

Inherently candid, Stevie had once confessed to him during a rambling conversation that she had a lamentable weakness for footloose artists and musicians, a penchant that had left her soft heart bruised more than once. He'd gotten the message, whether intentional or not on her part. Reclusive computer geeks were not her type romantically, though she seemed pleased to have one among her many pals.

Since she'd split with Joe, she'd been slightly more subdued than usual, but tonight she seemed even more dispirited. Had she been crying because she was lonely? Or—he swallowed hard, very much disliking the other possibility—because she missed the guy who'd caused her so much grief before he'd left town to start a new single life in Texas?

He tried to think of something more to say, but small talk wasn't his forte. Stevie usually carried their conversations, chattering away while he enjoyed listening and responding when prompted. Yet she never seemed bored by him, another trait that made her so special. Stevie would never yawn and check her watch during dinner with him.

He winced as he remembered the recent blind date he'd been stupid enough to consent to after being nagged by a friend's wife. He'd been just as disinterested during the evening, but he'd at least had the courtesy to not be so obvious about it. When he wanted to spend time with a woman, he had a few numbers he could call, a couple of women friends who wanted nothing more from him than a few hours of mutual pleasure. He didn't make those calls often—and even less so during the past couple of months, for some reason.

He didn't know why his mind had drifted in that direction at the moment, though the thought of dinner gave him inspiration. "Have you eaten?" he asked Stevie. "I've been on a plane all afternoon and I'm hungry."

She hesitated, then smiled a bit more naturally. "No, actually, I haven't had dinner. I might have even skipped lunch. I don't remember."

The admission made him even more convinced that something was troubling her, but he figured she'd tell him when and if she was ready. Maybe over a hot meal.

"I froze portions of that big pot of soup you made for me last week. It'll take just a few minutes to thaw and heat a couple bowlfuls."

She smoothed her tousled hair with one hand and

nodded. "Sounds good. Just let me wash up and I'll help you."

"I'll meet you in the kitchen."

Hastily stashing his bags to unpack later, he busied himself preparing the impromptu meal. Had he found the empty house he'd expected when he'd returned, he'd have nuked the soup and eaten in front of the TV with a beer straight from the can. But since he had company, he made more effort, setting the table with placemats and flatware, making sure the bowls weren't scratched or chipped.

For the most part, he'd learned to be content with his quiet life, so why was he so pleased by the prospect of sharing a simple bowl of soup with Stevie on a bleak, winter evening?

After splashing water on her face in Cole's guest bathroom, Stevie pressed a hand to her still-flat stomach, drew a deep breath and assured herself she looked reasonably presentable considering she'd just been startled out of a sound sleep. She seemed to be sleepy a lot these days. She hadn't even heard Cole enter the house.

The thought of him standing there watching her sleep made her pulse flutter. She supposed it was embarrassment at being caught off guard in his living room. He didn't seem to mind that she'd made herself at home while he was away, but then, she wouldn't have expected anything different from laid-back Cole.

In the year she'd known him, she'd never seen him rattled. She'd rarely observed any display of strong emotions from him, actually. He was the steadiest, most sensible person she knew, a calming presence in her sometimes hectic life. Maybe that was why she'd instinctively taken refuge in his living room when she'd been sad and stressed, though her cat-sitting duties had made a convenient excuse.

She scrutinized her reflection in the mirror. Had Cole seen the tear stains on her cheeks? She thought maybe he had and felt the heat of embarrassment. Though she wasn't usually shy about expressing her emotions— even tended to overshare at times—Stephanie "Stevie" McLane liked to think of herself as resilient, feisty and courageous. Not the type to hide in a friend's house and sniffle into his cat's soft fur. Still, Cole had merely searched her face with his dark, perceptive eyes, calmly asked if everything was okay, then offered her a hot meal. Somehow he'd seemed to know it was exactly what she'd needed, and not just because she was hungry.

He glanced up with a smile when she joined him in the kitchen. His thick, wavy dark hair was a bit messy, but then it always was. A hint of evening stubble shadowed his firm jaw. His eyes were the color of rich, dark chocolate. She'd always thought those beautiful eyes gleamed with both kindness and intelligence. Broad-shouldered and solidly built, he was not what she would call classically handsome, nor did he have that somewhat ethereal artist quality she'd always been drawn to in the past. He didn't talk a lot, and he wasn't prone to sharing his feelings. Still, there was something about Cole that automatically evoked trust and confidence.

She'd liked him from the day he'd moved into this house. There'd been a definite tug of feminine interest, but within her first hour of chatting with him— okay, interrogating him, as he'd humorously referred to that initial conversation—she'd found out he was a computer whiz, a widower and a country music fan who usually listened to news radio in his car. He was practically her total opposite, a stalwart Taurus to her capricious Gemini.

She'd tried to convince herself since then that her latent fascination with him was due more to those intriguing differences than to an underlying attraction she couldn't entirely deny. Despite being involved in an on-again, off-again relationship with a commitment-phobic musician for most of the time she'd known Cole, she'd have to have been brainless not to notice what a great guy he was. So different from her other male acquaintances, he was an enigma to her in many ways, but still they'd become friends. Maybe they could have become more than friends, had circumstances developed differently. She always enjoyed hanging out with him, and she missed him when he was away.

She had missed his steady, solid presence even more than usual during the past few days.

With old-fashioned courtesy, he held her chair for her as she took her seat at the table. "I don't have much to offer by way of a beverage," he said apologetically. "I can make coffee or there's beer or I can open a bottle of wine…"

"This is fine, thank you," she said, motioning toward the water glass he'd already filled and set beside her steaming bowl.

To quickly distract herself from her problems, she picked up her spoon and asked, "How was your trip?"

Seated now across the table from her, he grimaced. "Let's just say it's a miracle I'm not spending tonight in jail rather than having a nice bowl of soup with you."

She smiled. "Annoying associates?"

"To quote my late country grandpa, a couple of them were as dumb as a bag of rocks."

That made her laugh. She always loved it when Cole

quoted his "country grandpa," who had apparently been a treasury of old adages. "Knowing you, I'm sure you were completely polite and patient with them."

"I don't know how patient I was, but I tried not to tell them what I really thought. They didn't even try to pay attention half the time, then complained because they missed a few important points. It gets frustrating. Which is one of the main reasons I prefer telecommuting to pointless meetings and endless deliberations."

As a busy kitchen designer, Stevie knew all about frustrating collaborations. "Totally understand. There are plenty of times I want to dump a pitcher of ice water over a superpicky client or a lazy subcontractor."

He chuckled. "I'm sure you're able to sweet-talk all of them into seeing things your way. That's a talent I don't have."

She had to concede that no one would describe Cole as a "sweet talker." Or a talker at all, for that matter. Still, when he did speak, he always had something interesting and thoughtful to contribute. She'd consulted him several times about perplexing business issues, and had valued his measured, practical advice.

Biting her lip, she wondered what he would say if she confided her current, very personal predicament. She clenched her fingers in her lap.

Cole cleared his throat. She glanced up to find him studying her face with those too-knowing eyes. "Your food is getting cold," he said quietly.

Had he sensed somehow that she'd hovered on the verge of another meltdown? Either way, his reminder had been just what she'd needed to bring her back from the edge. Gripping her spoon so tightly her knuckles whitened, she concentrated on the soup and the cheese and crackers he'd served with it. In an attempt to keep him—and maybe herself—diverted, she talked as she ate, babbling away about anything that randomly occurred to her.

Seeming to have little trouble following her rapid changes of topic, Cole finished his meal then pulled a bag of cookies from the pantry for dessert. She declined the offer, finishing her rapidly cooling soup between sentences while he munched a couple of Oreos.

When he finished, he carried his dishes to the sink, sidestepping the cat munching kibble from a bowl on the floor. Stevie helped him clear the table, smiling up at him as they reached at the same time to close the dishwasher door.

"Thank you, Cole."

"For the soup? Wasn't any trouble, I just warmed it up. You actually made it."

She gave him a fondly chiding look. "Not for the soup, though I guess I needed that. Mostly, thanks for the company and conversation. I needed that even more tonight."

Wiping his hands, he turned to face her with a slight smile on his firm lips. "I didn't say much."

"I didn't give you much chance."

"Well, no, but I'm used to that."

She giggled, pleased to feel like laughing now, even at her own expense. She reached up to pat his cheek. "Are you calling me a chatterbox?"

"Just stating facts." His rare, full grin lit his eyes and carved long dimples around his mouth. Tousled and scruffy after his long day, he looked…well, adorable. His evening beard tickled her palm, and the warmth of his skin tempted her to nestle closer to his solid strength to alleviate her own nervous chill.

A bit unnerved by the impulse, she dropped her hand

quickly and laced her fingers together. This was not the time to be distracted by the physical attraction that had always underscored her friendship with Cole, an attraction she'd always assured herself she had very good reasons to keep private.

"You've been traveling all day," she said, rallying her inner defenses and taking a step back. "I'm sure you're tired. I should go and let you relax."

"There's no rush. We could stream a movie or something. I think I have some popcorn."

Her smile felt a little tremulous. He was being so sweetly concerned about her, even though he hadn't a clue what was troubling her. He'd probably looked forward to crashing on his couch or bed when he'd returned from his business trip. Instead, he'd found himself preparing dinner for a surprise guest and offering to entertain her even longer in case she was still reluctant to return to her own empty house. Was it any wonder she considered him one of her dearest friends?

"Thanks, Cole, but I think I'll just turn in early."

He frowned. "What if your power goes out tonight? With the layer of ice underneath this snow, it's a definite possibility."

"I have plenty of blankets to snuggle under, a couple of good flashlights, and a gas stovetop for heating water for tea."

"Your phone is charged?"

"Almost completely. And I'll plug it in as soon as I get home."

He nodded, though he didn't look entirely reassured.

She slid her hands down her sides in a nervous gesture. "So…"

Just as Cole wasn't much of a "talker," he wasn't much of a "toucher," either. Casual hugs and pats didn't come naturally to him, the way they did for her. He never seemed to mind being on the receiving end, though he'd once teased her about patting his cat goodnight, then doing the same to him as she'd prepared to leave.

So, it surprised her a little when he rested a hand on her shoulder as he gazed somberly into her eyes. "You know, Stevie, I'm not much of a conversationalist, but you've told me more than once that I'm a very good listener. And I'm your friend. If there's anything at all I can do for you, I hope you'd feel comfortable telling me."

Though she tried to hold on to her composure, all it took was a slight squeeze of his fingers to make her eyes fill with tears. To her consternation, sobs burst from her chest as an overtaxed emotional dam finally gave way, and there seemed to be nothing she could do to stop them.

After only a heartbeat's hesitation, Cole stepped forward and gathered her into his arms. He patted her back somewhat awkwardly, a bewildered male response that only made her cry harder.

"Stevie, tell me. What's wrong?"

"I'm—" She choked, then blurted out, "I'm pregnant."

Cole's hand froze in midpat. Of all the answers he had imagined, that was the lowest on his list.

Her voice muffled by his shoulder, she spoke in a flood of jumbled words interspersed with gulping sobs. "I'm sorry. It's just that I haven't told anyone, not even my best friends. This has been building up for weeks, ever since I first suspected I was pregnant, but I didn't want to even think about it. I tried to believe it was just stress or miscalculation, but it's real, and now I'm almost three months along. Joe moved to Austin and I'm pretty sure he has another girlfriend there already. He said he doesn't want a kid and he'd be a terrible father, anyway. I'm not even brokenhearted about the breakup because it wasn't working out and neither of us was really happy. Still, my brother and I grew up without our fathers and I always said I'd never do that to a child and I can't believe I was so stupid at my age. I'll do my best to give my baby a happy childhood. I mean, I turned out okay, right? But the weather was terrible tonight and I was home all alone and I just wanted company, even if it was only your cat," she finished in a soft wail.

He followed the tangled monologue, but just barely. It was a lot of information to digest in a very short amount of time. Fortunately, interpreting massive amounts of data was what he did every day. Stevie was three months pregnant. Joe was out of the picture. Stevie planned to raise the child alone. And she was obviously scared spitless.

Because a calm tone usually trumped overwrought emotion, he asked, "Have you seen a doctor?"

She nodded into his shoulder. "Twice."

"Are you okay? Healthy?"

Her sniffles slowed and she bobbed her head again. "Both of us are."

Both. He swallowed at the reminder that he wasn't holding just Stevie. He couldn't think of anything reassuring to say, so he fell back on practicality. Reaching around her, he snagged a paper towel from the counter and offered it to her. "I don't have a clean handkerchief on me, but maybe you could make use of this?"

His prosaic offer seemed to jolt her out of her meltdown. She made what appeared to be a heroic attempt to get her emotions under control. When she raised her head slowly to look at him, her wet, vivid blue eyes looked huge against her pale skin. She clutched his shirt in both fists as though anchoring herself in a whirlwind. Drawing a deep, unsteady breath, she relaxed her grip, carefully smoothed his crumpled shirt and stepped out of his arms. He hovered close. She still looked fragile enough to collapse at his feet.

"I, um—" It seemed to annoy her that her words were interrupted by a little catch of her breath. She cleared her throat and said, "I'm sorry I fell apart on you. The words just started flooding out and I couldn't stop them."

"You needed to unload," he said simply.

"I guess you're right," she said after a few moments. "Like I said, I haven't told anyone except Joe and my doctor. I just... I didn't know what to say."

"Keeping it to yourself for so long had to have been hard for you." It must have been especially difficult for naturally forthcoming Stevie.

Wiping her cheeks with the paper towel, she nodded. "Especially with Jenny and Tess. They're my best friends and we tell each other everything. Or we always have until now. But Tess is busy planning her wedding and Jenny and Gavin have been trying to get pregnant ever since they got married. How can I tell her that I accidentally got knocked up by a guy she never really liked all that much, anyway?"

He filled a glass with water and handed it to her without comment. She accepted it with a nod of thanks and took a few sips. He was relieved to note that the color was returning to her face, that her hand was steadier when she set the glass on the counter.

She drew a deep, unsteady breath before speaking

again. "It was after Christmas when I first suspected I was pregnant, but another couple of weeks before I let myself believe it."

"Had to have been a shock to you." It had certainly stunned him.

"To say the least. I felt obligated to call Joe, but he made it clear he won't be involved, so I'm on my own, which is fine with me since I'm not interested in seeing him again. I mean, yeah, it was irresponsible of me, but I'm thirty-one, you know? I'll be thirty-two in May. I've always thought I'd have a baby someday, and this could be my best chance. I've completely sworn off stupid fairy-tale fantasies for the future. It's taken me way too long and too many heartaches to figure out that I have not a shred of good judgment when it comes to romance. I've always been drawn to the guys who are the least likely to settle down, and I've always ended up on the losing end. No more. I'll figure out a way to raise this child on my own. Sure, it'll be tough making my schedule work out for the next few months and budgeting my savings to tide us over during the time I'll have to take off for maternity leave. I mean, my business is still pretty new and this is like the worst time to try to juggle contracts and finances and time off, but somehow I'll—"

"More water?" He motioned toward the glass as her nervous babbling threatened to lead to tears again. It was obvious she was on to him.

Drawing in another long breath, she smiled a bit wryly as she shook her head. Dusty wound around her ankles and she reached down to give the cat an absent stroke before straightening to speak more calmly again. "So, here I am. Single and pregnant, just like my mother was twice in two years with my brother and then me.

I haven't been sick a day and my doctor says I'm very healthy and so is the baby. I guess hormones just got the best of me tonight. I'll be fine, really."

"I have no doubt of it," he said. "You'll be a good mother."

She moistened her lips. "You really think so?"

"Absolutely." She should know by now that he didn't say things he didn't mean.

Her smile was sweetly tremulous. "Thank you, Cole. For the dinner, for letting me cry all over you, for being such a good friend. And now I really am going to leave so you can rest."

A good friend. He could be that for her.

He wasn't entirely sure she should be alone in her agitated mood, but he figured she would decline if he tried again to detain her. So he merely nodded and said, "I'll walk you home."

Tossing the crumpled paper towel into the trash, she glanced over her shoulder with a lifted eyebrow. "Since when do you need to walk me next door?"

"Since there's ice all over the walkway and you're pregnant," he replied bluntly. "I want to make sure you don't fall."

"It's not necessary, but I can see you're going to insist." Her smile looked a bit more natural now, though still not the high-wattage grin he associated with her.

With a faint smile in return, he nodded. "You're right. I am."

Minutes later, bundled into their coats, they walked out into what amounted to an Arkansas blizzard. Snow fell so hard he could hardly see Stevie's white house on the big corner lot next door. The ground was already covered and no cars drove down the street, most of the locals having taken the advice of forecasters and burrowed safely into their homes for the night.

It wouldn't stay this peaceful, of course. He'd bet the generally well-behaved but exuberant Bristol kids across the street would be out playing in the snow as soon as their mom gave them permission. Snow days were always a rare treat around here, even though they proved a headache for road crews and first responders.

He kept his gaze trained on Stevie as they stepped off his porch. Her disposition changed the moment they moved out into the winter storm. She couldn't seem to resist turning her face up to let the snow fall against her cheeks. The security lamps above them provided just enough light for Cole to see the white flakes glittering on her skin and in her golden curls. With her signature musical laugh, she held out her arms and turned in a little circle, her shoes crunching on the thin layer of ice beneath the accumulating snow. Bemused by her mercurial mood shifts, and well aware they had more to do with her unique personality than to fluctuating hormones, he chuckled and caught her arm to make sure she didn't fall.

"Isn't it beautiful?" she asked with a sigh, wrapping her hands around his arm and smiling companionably up at him.

"Very."

Her lashes fluttered, though he wasn't sure whether that was due to the snow or his husky tone. He cleared his throat. He must be more tired than he'd realized, or more shaken than he'd have expected by Stevie's bombshell. Whatever the reason, he found himself wanting to prolong this cozy walk in the snowy night with Stevie tucked close to his side, breath clouds mingling and drifting in the air in front of them. For the second time in just over an hour, he felt almost as if he'd stepped into one of his private fantasies. He was glad mind reading wasn't among Stevie McLane's many talents. He wasn't sure how she'd react to knowing that just watching her catching a snowflake on her tongue sent his imagination down a path much more hazardous than the one on which they walked.

Burying those uncomfortable thoughts deep inside his mind, he made an effort to keep his expression blandly friendly until they were on her small porch. She unlocked the front door she'd painted bright blue to match the shutters. One hand on the knob, she smiled up at him. "Okay, I'm safely home. You can relax."

He searched her face in the soft glow of her porch light. "You're sure you're okay? If you need anything else this evening, even if just to talk more, I'm available."

In a gesture that was both impulsive and entirely characteristic, she wrapped her arms around his waist for a hug. "Thank you," she said. "You're a very nice man, Cole McKellar."

A very nice man. As flattering as her comments were, they were hardly the words she'd have whispered in one of those steamy daydreams. Giving himself a mental slap, he returned his friend's hug with a brief squeeze before stepping back. "Good night, Stevie. Call if you need me."

She opened her door. "Good night, Cole."

He stepped down from the little porch into the falling snow, which was already hiding the footprints they'd left on the way. He'd taken only a step when something made him turn back around. "Stevie?"

She paused in the act of closing the door. "Yes?"

"You aren't alone."

With that blurted promise, he turned and headed home, his head down, his fists shoved into the pockets of his coat. He'd taken quite a few steps by the time he heard Stevie close her door.

Chapter Two

Stevie woke late Saturday morning feeling more positive than she had since she first suspected she was pregnant. She wandered to her bedroom window to look over an expanse of glittering snow toward Cole's house. Simply sharing her predicament with him last night had seemed to take a load off her shoulders.

You aren't alone. She could still hear the echo of his deep voice. The words had lulled her to sleep last night, and were still drifting through her mind when she'd awakened. She couldn't begin to express how much it had meant to her to hear them.

Cole was such a great guy. Quiet, but with his own sly sense of humor. Fascinatingly intelligent, in a mathish sort of way. And completely nonjudgmental, a particularly appealing trait at the moment.

A habitual matchmaker for her friends, she'd occasionally tried to think of someone who'd be a good match for this supernice man, but for some reason she could never come up with anyone who seemed just right for him. A secret part of her had acknowledged on occasion that she'd selfishly wanted to keep him to herself. She had pushed that unsettling voice aside, reminding herself that she'd been in no position to make a play for Cole even if he'd encouraged her.

She wasn't even sure he'd dated seriously in the year she'd known him, though he went out sometimes in the evenings, casually alluding to gatherings with friends. He didn't talk about his late wife much, but on those rare occasions his face warmed and softened. She could tell he had truly loved her. Natasha had been gone for several years, but maybe he still mourned her too deeply to be interested in a new relationship. It was hard to be sure with Cole. He tended to keep his deepest emotions to himself.

It made her sad to think of him still grieving, unwilling or unable to fall in love again. Only because he was her friend and she wanted all her friends to be happy, she assured herself. Still, he seemed content with his home, a job he enjoyed and the friends she hadn't met, so maybe that was enough for him.

She dressed in jeans and a multicolored sweater with colorfully striped knee socks, figuring she'd be out in the cold at some point. As had been her habit the past couple weeks, she turned sideways in front of the mirror to check her figure. Her jeans were getting a little snug in the waist and her bras were a bit tight on her already-generous bustline, but she doubted even her closest friends would be able to guess her condition by looking at her.

She must tell Tess and Jenny soon. She felt incredibly guilty that she hadn't already, even more than not having told her mother and brother. Her two closest friends would forgive her, would even understand why she'd kept her secret for so long, but she wouldn't blame them if they were a bit hurt, at least at first. Especially Jenny, who'd been her best friend since their school days. They'd met Tess almost two years ago and they'd been a tight trio ever since, though they couldn't spend quite as much time together now that Jenny was married and Tess was busily planning a June wedding.

Being human, after all, and the most unabashedly romantic of the small group, Stevie couldn't help feeling a little envious that both Jenny and Tess had found the loves of their lives while her own romances always fizzled. Perhaps she'd been destined all along to follow in her mother's self-reliant footsteps. Was it in her genes to habitually fall for the men who were least likely to settle down to marriage and families?

Shaking her head in exasperation, she turned away from the window.

After eating breakfast, she went into a spare bedroom she used as a home office. Sitting at her desk, she thought of Cole. Like him, she worked from home a lot, but she also leased a small office in a midtown strip center, though most of her work hours were spent in on-site meetings with clients. She was glad she had a third bedroom so she wouldn't lose her office when the baby came.

She'd been at it only an hour when she was interrupted by the chime of the doorbell. Glancing at the clock, she saw that it was just after eleven. She wasn't expecting anyone. Thinking Cole had come over to check on her, she opened the door with an eager smile that wavered only a little when she saw the caller.

"Hi, guys, what's up?" she asked the three pink-cheeked, heavily bundled kids grinning up at her. The Bristol siblings were cute little peas from the same pod, all red-haired, green-eyed and snub-nosed. The boys, Leo and Asher, were nine and seven. Charlotte was five. Baby sister Everly—the "surprise baby," according to their mother, Lori—was presumably at home with their mom. A rather chaotic pathway of little footprints in the snow led from their house across the cul-de-sac to Stevie's small porch.

"Can you come out and help us build a snowman, Miss Stevie?" Charlotte asked with wide, hopeful eyes. "Mommy's taking care of Everly and Daddy's at work."

She wasn't surprised by the request. Since the baby's birth six months ago, she'd played with them several times to give their somewhat harried mother a few minutes to rest on days when her firefighter husband was on twenty-four-hour shifts. They'd thrown basketballs at the hoop mounted above their garage door, played tag and catch, even sat at the picnic table in their backyard with board games. Lori had been almost tearfully grateful for the breaks, but Stevie never minded. She liked kids, particularly these funny and well-behaved siblings.

"Give me five minutes to bundle up and I'll join you in your yard."

The children cheered happily.

"Leo, hold Charlotte's hand on the way back across the street," she instructed. "And look both ways before you cross."

Leo made an exaggerated show of taking his little sister's hand to lead her across the empty street to their own yard. Smiling, Stevie closed her door and turned toward the bedroom.

Half an hour later, she was breathless and covered

with snow from the bright blue knit cap on her head to the waterproof pink boots into which she'd tucked her jeans. Her hooded jacket was yellow, her gloves the same blue as her hat. Charlotte told her she looked like she was wearing a rainbow. Laughing, Stevie showed her how to make a snow angel, adding to her frosty coating.

With the thin layer of sleet beneath, the snow crunched when they played in it. Gray clouds hung low above them, but happy laughter reigned in the Bristol's front yard. From inside the warm house, Lori and baby Everly appeared occasionally in a window to watch, and Stevie waved to them. Next year that little angel, too, would be out playing in the snow. And she would have a baby of her own to watch, she realized with a hard thump of her heart. To soothe the fresh attack of nerves, she focused on the Bristol kids.

The boys had nearly cleared the front lawn of packable snow in the quest to make their snowman "supersized." It was so big that Stevie was elected to lift the giant head onto the body. She drew a deep breath and prepared to give it her best shot. Two strong, black-gloved hands came from behind her to offer assistance. She looked over her shoulder and smiled when she saw Cole standing there. He wore a black watchman cap over his thick dark hair, a black jacket and black boots—a more somber, coordinated ensemble than her own.

His chocolate eyes gleamed with amusement as he grinned down at her. "Need a hand?"

"Or two," she agreed. "These kids like their snowmen on the larger side."

"We're building a snow giant!" Asher exclaimed eagerly, carrying a large stick he'd found in the backyard. "This can be one of his arms. Leo's looking for another."

With Cole's help, they made short work of completing their snow friend, accessorizing with a battered ball cap and frayed scarf donated by Lori. They created facial features with decorative river rocks filched from the flower beds. It had started to snow again, to the children's delight. Another half inch was predicted on top of the six inches that had collected during the night. Stevie figured the snowman would survive a day or two before the warmer temperatures forecast for later in the week melted him away.

After being summoned for lunch by their mother, the siblings politely thanked Stevie and Cole for their assistance in building "the best snowman ever!" They tramped reluctantly inside their house when their mother called out again. Stevie grimaced sympathetically as she imagined the wet mess of clothing and puddles Lori would deal with, but maybe the busy mom would consider it a fair trade-off for the hour of volunteer babysitting. From the open doorway, with Everly on her hip, she called out an offer of hot chocolate, but they declined cordially.

"Though, actually, hot chocolate sounds like a good idea," Stevie confided to Cole as they tramped across the street. She wiped snowflakes from her eyelashes with the back of one damp glove. "I'm freezing."

"Your jeans are wet from rolling around in the snow with Charlotte. You should get into dry clothes."

She noted he'd stayed much drier, maybe because he'd been a little less enthusiastic about getting down in the snow, she admitted with a grin.

"Come in, if you have time," she said, motioning toward her house. "I make a mean mug of cocoa."

"That sounds really—"

His right foot slipped on a slick spot on her driveway. Flailing comically, he went down flat on his back in the snow. Stevie almost burst into laughter at the funny expression he made as he lay there, but she managed to contain her amusement to a grin.

"Are you hurt?" she asked, though she could tell at a glance that he'd damaged only his pride.

Very deliberately, he spread his arms and legs into Vs, then climbed to his feet, surveying the resulting snow angel with a nod of satisfaction. "I meant to do that."

Delighted by his quick wit, she laughed and tucked a hand companionably beneath his arm. "Let's go get warm."

"Sounds good to me," he said, covering her hand with his own. And though they both wore gloves, she could still feel the warmth of his touch spreading through her.

Having shed their wet boots on the porch, Cole insisted that Stevie change into dry clothes before she played hostess. She left him to wash up in the guest bath while she ducked into her bedroom to change into a loose sweater and leggings. Fluffing her curls with her hands, she gave herself a quick once-over in the full-length, silver-framed, art deco mirror that coordinated with her sage, silver and cream French deco bedroom furnishings. Her cheeks and nose were still pink from the cold but she resisted an impulse to touch up her minimal makeup for her guest's benefit. After all, it was just Cole, right?

Her country French kitchen was her favorite room in the house. The walls were warm sage, the cabinets knotty pecan with leaded glass inserts, the counters brown-and-tan granite with antique bronze hardware. Cole joined her there, looking casually at ease in his sweater, jeans and wool socks. His dark hair was disheveled from the hat he'd removed, and her fingers itched with a sudden urge to play in those thick, unruly waves. She opened the refrigerator instead. "How about a sandwich before we drink our cocoa? Playing in the snow always gives me an appetite."

"Sounds good, if it's not too much trouble. What can I do to help?"

When they sat down to lunch, to her relief, he didn't bring up her pregnancy. He merely ate his grilled cheddar-and-tomato sandwiches and munched salt-and-vinegar chips while she babbled nervously about everything and anything—except her predicament.

After the dishes were cleared away, they moved to the living room with steaming cups of cocoa topped with marshmallows. She'd indulged her love of eclectic European and American deco design in here, too. Flames crackled among the gas logs in the fireplace framed in white-painted carved wood, spreading warmth through the room. With her feet curled comfortably beneath her, she sat on the dove-gray couch that faced the fireplace. Cole had settled in a tapestry armchair near her end of the couch. She couldn't help admiring the way the firelight brought out the highlights in his hair.

"I've always liked this room," he commented, stretching his legs in front of him toward the fire. "It always impresses me that it can look so classy yet still be so comfortable. Not fussy and formal like some people's decorated places."

Pleased by the comments, she beamed. "That's exactly what I aim for in my decorating. Stylish, but welcoming. Home design is meant to be enjoyed. Lived in, not just admired or photographed."

He nodded in approval. "That's as it should be. I've always said it was a waste to have furniture you can't sit on or carpet you feel guilty walking on. Tasha—"

He stopped talking and took a sip of his cocoa.

She swirled her beverage gently in her mug to better distribute the melting marshmallows. "Natasha agreed with your design aesthetic?" she prodded gently. She was curious to hear more about the woman he'd married, but she didn't want to cause him pain talking about her.

He shrugged, his expression wry. "She wasn't really into decorating. As long as she had a comfortable chair for reading, she was happy."

"She liked to read?"

"Almost obsessively, especially as her health declined and there was little else she could do."

"Was she sick for a long time?"

"Yes," he replied quietly.

And Cole had taken care of her during that time. She had no doubt that Natasha had received the best of care from him. Unlike most of the men in her own past, Cole wasn't the type to walk away from his responsibilities and commitments, even when those challenges were daunting. Any woman who captured his heart would be very fortunate, indeed, she thought a bit wistfully.

"Do you have plans for the day?" he asked, and it couldn't be more obvious that he wanted to change the subject.

She obliged. "I was going to spend a few hours at my office, but I think I'll just work at home this afternoon instead, considering drivers around here go insane when there's snow on the roads."

"Good plan. So, are you, um, feeling better today?"

She managed not to grimace in response to the oblique reminder of last night's meltdown, but it still embarrassed her. "Much better, thank you. I had fun playing with the Bristol kids this morning."

"Nice kids. They're obviously crazy about you."

"I like them, too."

He finished his cocoa. A dab of marshmallow dotted his upper lip when he lowered the mug. She eyed it from beneath her lashes. She wasn't sure why she wasn't teasing him about it. Normally she would have, but something held her back just then. Maybe it was the crazy image that popped unexpectedly into her head—herself licking away that tempting smudge and then sampling the taste of chocolate on his firm lips.

She blinked rapidly, shocked at the direction her thoughts had taken. *Hormones.* That had to be the explanation. Sure, she'd always been aware of Cole as an attractive man, not to mention his other fine qualities, but she'd deliberately avoided thinking of him in that way. She'd made some really bad decisions when it came to romance, leading, if not to heartbreak, at least to frequent disappointment. Tragically widowed, Cole had shown so signs that he wanted more from her than friendship. And besides, she treasured their relationship too much to risk ruining it by trying to convince themselves they were a compatible match. Most especially not now, considering her awkward predicament.

He wiped off that distracting bit of marshmallow with a napkin, then stood to carry his mug to the kitchen. She followed with her own. He turned just as she approached the sink, and they very nearly collided. With a low laugh, he caught her shoulders. "Steady there."

Heat flared from his touch. For a moment, her mind went blank. She took a jerky step backward, then tried to cover her discomfiture with a laugh. "Were you afraid I was going to knock you over?"

He smiled. "Maybe. I've already landed at your feet once in the past twenty-four hours. And there's no snow in here to give me a credible reason for being on the ground."

She laughed and moved to rinse her mug in the sink. When she turned back around, she found Cole looking up at her high ceiling with a frown. "You have a bulb out," he said.

She followed his glance and saw the dark bulb in one of the recessed canisters that provided auxiliary lighting to the pendant lamps over the island. "I thought something looked different in that corner."

"Do you have a spare bulb?"

"Yes. I'll change it later."

He was shaking his head before she'd completed the sentence. "You don't need to climb ladders in your condition. I'll take care of it."

She had to admit it was difficult for her, at five-two, to change the bulbs in her nine-foot kitchen ceiling. Grateful for his assistance, she fetched a bulb and a stepladder, then turned off the light switch. She leaned against a nearby counter while Cole climbed onto the stepladder and reached overhead. For a self-professed "computer nerd," the man did stay in good condition, she thought, watching muscles ripple as he stretched upward and his shirt exposed part of what looked to be a perfectly formed six pack.

"Well, damn."

She lifted an eyebrow in response to his growl. "What's wrong?"

"Bulb broke off in my hand and now the cap's stuck in the socket."

"Hang on, I'll grab a potato."

He stepped off the ladder to toss the broken bulb into the trash, watching while she sliced a fat potato neatly in half. "So you know that trick."

She smiled as she handed him one half of the potato. "I've broken a few bulbs in my time. My mom taught me this trick years ago. Our budget was usually tight, so she was the 'handyman' around here when we were growing up, at least until my brother and I were old enough to do our share of maintenance."

"She sounds very self-sufficient."

"I suppose she had to be. I've told you, of course, that Mom never married the fathers of either of her kids. She had issues with commitment, and she said neither of them were the home-and-hearth types, anyway. My father died when I was just a toddler, leaving nothing for my support. Mom didn't get much help from my brother's dad, either, but she supported us well enough on her own. She put a down payment on this house with a small inheritance from her parents when Tom and I were very young, and then paid it off over the next ten years with her salary. She was a shrewd budgeter. She gave us a good home here—even though working nine to five in a state job smothered her gypsy soul, as she informed us too many times to count."

Back up on the ladder, Cole glanced down at her when she stopped for a breath. "She sounds like a unique woman."

She smiled. "She is that."

Practically the day Stevie had graduated from college, her accomplished but unconventional mother had announced she was retiring from her job with the state and moving to Hawaii. Upon her retirement, she'd sold Stevie this house for a bargain price and had gone off to find herself on a warm beach.

She turned to pull a bottle of water from the fridge, speaking almost to herself as she twisted off the cap. "I only hope I can handle the challenges of single mother-hood as well as Mom did."

"You'll be great." He pushed the potato into the broken bulb and twisted. The resulting metallic squeal made them both grimace, but the trick worked. Stevie held up a wastebasket for the potato and broken parts, then handed him the new bulb.

"Thanks," he said, reaching up again before asking in a conversational tone, "Do you remember your fa-ther at all?"

"No. Like I said, I was just a toddler when he was killed in a car wreck, and he'd never even seen me."

"And your brother's father?"

"Tom's dad is still living, as far as we know, but they've never had a relationship. It was just the three of us here."

She gave a little sigh. "I have to admit I was always envious of my friends who had fathers in their lives. Jenny grew up without a dad, too, so she and I bonded in childhood over that, but we were both a little jeal-ous of the girls who had dads to take them to father-daughter dances or even to give their boyfriends the third degree," she added with a rueful laugh. "I know Tom would have liked having a father to play catch with him and take him fishing and other male bond-ing stuff. Mom threw a mean curve ball and taught us to ride our bikes and drive and do basic home and car maintenance, everything we needed, really…but I've always thought if I ever had a kid, I'd give him or her the one thing missing from my own otherwise happy childhood. A dad."

Dusting off his hands, Cole climbed down and folded the stepladder. "Not everyone is lucky enough to have a close relationship with their father," he muttered as he carried the ladder toward the laundry room.

She watched him thoughtfully. Though he hadn't said much about his family issues, she knew Cole wasn't close to his father. He'd told her his parents were divorced, and both remarried. His mother had moved to another state several years ago, and he'd spent most of his childhood with his paternal grandparents—the "country grandpa" he quoted often—but he hadn't given details of his estrangement from his dad.

Maybe it was just as well she was doing this on her own, she thought with a sigh. Her child's biological father had no interest at all in fatherhood. Had she been with someone different, someone more steady and reliable and responsible—someone like Cole, she thought with a hard swallow—well, that could have had a very different outcome.

Rejoining her, Cole glanced around the kitchen. "Is there anything else I can do for you before I go? Any more repairs you need seen to? It's the least I can do in return for all the cat sitting you're doing this week."

She smiled. "No, that's it, thanks."

"You have food and supplies so you don't have to go out this afternoon? The roads are still a mess."

She patted his arm. "I'm good, Cole, thank you."

He caught her hand in his, gave the fingers a little squeeze, then released her quickly and took a step back. "I'd better go, then. I have a conference call later this afternoon and I need to get ready for it."

"You have a conference call on a Saturday afternoon?" she asked as she followed him into the living room.

He reached for his coat and hat. "Yeah. A lot going on with work this week. I'll probably be tied up for a couple hours, but if you need anything don't hesitate to let me know, okay?"

"I'll be fine. Be careful walking home. I think we have enough snow angels out there."

He made a face that drew a laugh from her. "I'll watch my step."

His faint smile fading, he paused with his hand on the doorknob, looking as though there was something on his mind. Her fingers laced tightly in front of her. She waited, but he remained silent.

His gaze lifted, locking with hers. Lost in his bottomless dark eyes, she stared back at him. It felt as though something important hovered between them, but she couldn't quite figure out what it was. Something he wanted to say? To do? Something he was waiting for her to say or do?

"Call if you need me," he said and opened the door. He was gone before she could even respond.

Biting her lip, she locked the door behind him, then crossed the room and sank onto the couch. Something had changed between her and Cole since she'd shared her news with him, she thought wistfully. She couldn't define it, exactly. Cole certainly wasn't showing disapproval. Just the opposite, in fact; he'd been supportive and considerate. He'd sounded sincere when he said he had faith in her. As the first of her friends she'd told, he'd reacted exactly the way she hoped they all would.

And yet, something was different. She could only describe it as an awareness she hadn't acknowledged before. Whether it was only on her part, she couldn't say, but what else could it be? Maybe it was all in her head. Maybe those wonky hormones and jumbled emotions were making her imagine things that weren't real. Whatever the reason, she had to get a grip. She'd made quite a few foolish mistakes in the past few months, but she would never do anything that would put her treasured friendship with Cole at risk.

Her phone rang some three hours after Cole left. Looking away from the kitchen design on her computer monitor, she glanced at the ID screen on her phone. She smiled when she saw Cole's name. Was he checking on her again already? Very sweet, but she'd have to convince him she was fine so he would stop worrying about her. It hadn't helped, of course, that she'd blubbered all over him last night, she thought with a wince.

With that embarrassing memory in mind, she answered cheerily. "Hi, Cole. What's up?"

"Just letting you know I'm going to have to catch a plane to Chicago first thing in the morning."

She frowned. "I thought you weren't leaving until later in the week."

"So did I. But the conference call I mentioned was a nightmare. I have to go sort out some stuff. And try not to knock heads together while I'm there," he finished grimly.

She giggled, but a bit wistfully. He'd only just gotten back from the last trip. She wished he didn't have to go again so soon. She was sure he felt the same way, though probably not for the same reasons. "I'll take good care of Dusty."

"You always do. I'm pretty sure you're her favorite person. Which I understand completely," he added, and she could hear the smile in his voice now.

"Why, thank you, kind sir."

His low chuckle rumbled pleasantly in her ear. "The roads should be much better tomorrow, but don't take any chances, okay? Be careful."

"I will. You do the same."

She set her phone aside with a little sigh after they disconnected. She would miss him again. But maybe it would be good to have a little distance from him for a few days. She was quite sure everything would be back to normal—as much as possible considering the circumstances, anyway—once he returned.

It had been a long, frustrating day, but that wasn't what kept Cole awake Tuesday night. Ultimately, the business problems had been settled to everyone's satisfaction, and he would be able to return to Little Rock Thursday and get back to work in his much-preferred home office. So, it wasn't the job that had him tossing and turning in the hotel bed, or that made him finally give up and move to the window to stare blankly out at the midnight Chicago skyline. His thoughts were several hundred miles away. With Stevie McLane, to be precise.

Even when he'd been immersed in discussions about figures and trends and mathematical models, he'd been aware of thoughts of her hovering at the back of his mind, ready to push to the forefront as soon as he was alone. It was rare that he allowed himself to be distracted from work, but he hadn't been able to stop thinking about Stevie since she'd confided her pregnancy to him Friday night. He'd acknowledged privately that Stevie had been in his thoughts increasingly often during the past months, but even more so this week.

Something she'd said Saturday kept replaying in his

mind. *I've always thought if I ever had a kid, I'd give him or her the one thing missing from my own otherwise happy childhood. A dad.*

A brainstorm had occurred to him in the middle of that night, and he'd been pondering it ever since, giving it his usual thorough contemplation of all potential consequences. He still had nagging doubts about whether he was qualified to even make the offer, considering the poor example his own father had set, but he'd decided he should at least discuss the idea with Stevie.

He wasn't sure which possible outcome unnerved him most. That she would turn him down…or that she would accept.

He turned away from the window and padded back over to the tousled bed. He always kept a few interesting nonfiction books on his tablet. Maybe if he read awhile, he'd lull himself to sleep. Reaching out to turn on the bedside lamp, he muttered a curse when he knocked his wallet off the nightstand. He reached down to scoop it up and it fell open in his hands. He started to close it when something made him pause. Very slowly, he reached into the back of the wallet and drew out a small photograph with worn edges.

He'd once commented to Natasha that she had the face of a Renaissance Madonna. She'd laughed and told him not to be silly, but that hadn't changed the fact that she could have posed for one of those famous paintings. Framed by straight, dark hair, her oval face had been delicate, her skin a flawless olive. Her dark hazel eyes had been striking in their intensity and clarity, making him feel at times as though she could see right into him. Despite that serene exterior, she'd had a warrior spirit, refusing to accept the health issues that had eventually led to her death. She'd made plans for a long marriage, for a career, for a family. She'd clung to those dreams until the very end of her life.

He ran his fingertips slowly across the face in the photo. Natasha had been gone five years, leaving him a widower before he'd turned thirty. She wouldn't have wanted him to spend the rest of his life alone. But still, he felt a niggle of remorse whenever he envisioned himself having all the things she had wanted so badly and would never have.

She would understand, he told himself, sliding the photo back into place. She'd have liked Stevie, though they had little in common other than kind hearts and innate optimism. Natasha would certainly understand his compulsion to offer assistance to a valued friend, someone in a difficult situation. She had once described him as a compulsive caregiver.

His growing attraction to Stevie during the past year had made him both uncomfortable and vaguely guilty, despite his assurances of what Tasha would have wanted for him. He'd thought it a futile fantasy, a sometimes-lonely bachelor's natural infatuation for a desirable and fascinating woman. But now Stevie's circumstances had taken a daunting turn. And he'd promised her she wouldn't be alone.

Maybe he could give Stevie what he had failed to provide for Natasha no matter how hard he'd tried, he thought bleakly, tossing the wallet aside. Moving to stare out the window again, he wished he could erase the nagging apprehension that he didn't have enough to offer.

After several business meetings Monday and another appointment with her obstetrician Tuesday, Stevie spent Wednesday evening relaxing with her friends

Jenny Locke and Tess Miller for an ever-more-rare girls' night out. In addition to their changing personal lives, all of them stayed busy with their successful careers. Jenny owned two fashion and accessories boutiques and planned to open another within the next year. Tess was the office manager for her fiancé's thriving commercial construction company. Stevie's kitchen design business was growing increasingly in demand due to recommendations from her satisfied customers. It was getting harder all the time to find a night when all three were free, but they made an effort to nurture the friendship that meant so much to all of them.

They enjoyed gathering occasionally at Jenny's boutique, Complements, after business hours. With no other customers in the store, Stevie and Tess could try on new outfits, play with the latest bags and jewelry and supplement their wardrobes with the "friends and family discount" Jenny always extended to them. Tonight they huddled around a counter spread with magazines, photographs and fabric samples Tess had brought with her. Two computer tablets lay amongst the clutter, different bridal websites displayed on the screens.

"So, we all agree?" Tess asked. "We like these colors? Poppy red and pale yellow? And what about the bridesmaids' dresses? Is there any particular style you both prefer?"

Stevie bit her lip as she did a quick mental calculation. Tess's wedding was scheduled for mid-June. Stevie would be seven months pregnant and sporting a big belly by then. It was time to come clean with her friends. She didn't know why it was so much harder to confide in them than it had been with Cole. She was sure Jenny and Tess were going to be supportive, though she wouldn't be surprised if tears were shed, and not all of them hers. She drew a deep breath.

"Hello?" Tess studied both Stevie and Jenny with a quizzical expression. "Neither of you is answering me. Which style do you like for the bridesmaids' dresses?"

Jenny spoke before Stevie had a chance to share her news. "Um, Tess? If it's okay with you, I think we should choose a loose, nonfitted style."

Something in Jenny's tone made both Stevie and Tess look at her curiously. Her expression made Stevie's breath catch, and she heard Tess give a little squeak.

"Jen?" Tess's voice was breathless with anticipation.

A shaky smile spread across Jenny's beautiful face. "I'm pregnant."

The words Stevie had been prepared to say lodged in her throat.

Jenny looked at Tess when she added, "I'm only four weeks along, so I'm a little nervous about even mentioning it yet. But with the wedding preparations moving along, and the need to order dresses soon, I thought you should know now."

Tess squealed and reached out to her friend. Though usually the most exuberantly demonstrative of the trio, Stevie paused a beat before throwing herself into the group hug. She hoped her hesitation, if noticed, would be attributed to happy surprise.

Jenny was already answering a barrage of questions from Tess. Yes, she felt fine other than some morning nausea; yes, Gavin was super excited; yes, they'd told their families and everyone was thrilled.

Swiping at her damp cheeks, Tess beamed and started gathering the wedding materials. "All of this can wait. Let's go to the restaurant next door and we can talk about your news over dinner. I want to hear how your mom and grandmother reacted. I know Gavin's big family must have gone crazy. Do you know when you'll start decorating the nursery? I bet Stevie can help you with that, can't you, Stevie?"

"Well, I'm more comfortable with kitchens, but I'm sure I can come up with a few suggestions for decorating a nursery." Stevie smiled brightly as she set her own momentous news aside for now. Jenny glowed with happiness about her pregnancy, and Tess was still eager to discuss the simple, but certain-to-be-beautiful wedding she was trying to put together quickly. This seemed entirely the wrong time to mention that she was already three months pregnant herself.

She hid her inner turmoil for the remainder of the evening behind mile-a-minute chatter and animated laughter, giving her friends little opportunity to ask anything personal of her. They had an absolutely delightful evening, yet Stevie had trouble fully enjoying it.

"I just couldn't tell them," she said to Cole the next afternoon, restlessly pacing her living room. "Jenny was so happy to make her announcement—and very nervous that it's still early so something could yet go wrong. And Tess is focusing on her wedding arrangements. She's seeing everything through orange blossom-colored lenses right now. If I'd told them my situation, they'd have started worrying about me and obsessing about my situation rather than their own excitement and I didn't want our special evening to veer off into that direction last night, so I—"

"Breathe, Stevie." Watching her from an armchair, Cole broke in to interrupt the rush of words she'd been holding in for hours. His deep voice was a soothing balm to her frayed nerves. "You'll hyperventilate."

He'd arrived only a few minutes earlier to let her

know he was back in town and thank her, as he always did, for taking care of Dusty while he was gone. Stevie had barely waited until he was seated before she'd started pacing and venting to the only person who truly understood what she'd been going through recently.

She inhaled deeply. Staying busy with work, she'd held herself together pretty well since she'd parted from her friends last night with warm hugs and too-bright smiles, but just seeing Cole on her doorstep had brought her emotions dangerously close to the surface again. She paused in front of him, pushed her hair from her face with both hands and managed a smile of sorts.

"Sorry. I don't mean to keep unloading all my problems on you. It's your fault for being such a good listener," she added, trying to lighten the mood with teasing.

"I don't mind," he assured her, and made her believe him. "Actually, I've given your situation a great deal of thought, and I have some suggestions for you, if you're interested in hearing them."

He looked so solemn that she had to smile despite her agitation. "You've given this careful consideration, have you?"

His lips twitched. "I've analyzed the data you presented to me and I would like to suggest some viable alternatives for your consideration."

She chuckled in response to his self-mocking expression, then grew serious again. "That's very sweet of you, but I'm sure I'll work out a plan of some sort."

His faint smile vanished. "You're stressed, and that's not good for either you or the baby. I understand why you were reluctant to talk to your girlfriends last night, under the circumstances, and apparently you aren't quite ready to turn to your family. But I'm your friend, too, and I'm here for you. This is what I do, you know. I look at all the angles of a problem and identify solutions."

She twisted a shoulder-length curl around her finger in her habitual nervous gesture. "I know you're a genius at your work. But I'm not sure my current situation is in your wheelhouse."

"Not exactly, but I'd like to try to help. I made a few notes." He reached into his shirt pocket, drawing out his ever-present, tablet-sized smartphone. He pushed a button, then studied the words on the screen intently.

Seriously? He'd made notes? Was this the cutest thing ever?

"You said you didn't want to raise your child without a father. Is there any chance the biological father will change his mind about being involved?"

"None," she said with absolute certainty, amusement evaporating. "He made that very clear."

Cole nodded, then moved on to his next point. "You said you worried about keeping your business afloat, both financially and logistically, while juggling maternity leave and infant care."

"That will be a challenge," she admitted, twisting the curl more tightly. "I've already started saving as much as I can stash away and I'm trying to keep my calendar organized around my due date."

"You're going to need help," he said bluntly. "I believe there's an obvious solution. The ideal option is for you to marry someone who likes and wants kids. Someone who can help you with the myriad daily responsibilities of raising a child and running a successful business."

Taken aback, she shook her head in bemusement. This was the strategy Cole thought was obvious? That she should simply find someone to marry before her baby's arrival?

"Cole, that's—"

He seemed intent on quickly spelling out his reasoning. "You said you're done with unstable romances. I'm of the opinion, myself, that marriages built on practical foundations are more sustainable than those based on fantasy and infatuation. My parents, for example, married in a youthful whirlwind romance that ended in a bitter and acrimonious divorce. Both wed for the second time for far more sensible purposes and those marriages have been much more successful."

"You're suggesting I should marry a friend to help me raise my child?"

Cole nodded, looking for all the world as if his improbable conclusion made perfect sense. He set aside the phone. "It's the ideal solution."

She gave him a quizzical smile. "So, are *you* offering to marry me, Cole?"

His look of surprise almost made her laugh again. He must not have realized how his suggestion could be interpreted, she mused in fond indulgence.

"I thought you understood," he said, his expression very earnest now. "That's exactly what I'm doing."

Chapter Three

Stevie's soft laughter ended with a choke. She coughed a couple of times, waving Cole off when he stood and stepped forward as if to pound her back. Once she'd recovered her breath, she told herself she must have misheard him. "You, um—what?"

"I'm asking you to marry me," he repeated. Slowly this time, as if to make sure she comprehended.

Though her first reaction was shock, as his words sank in she found herself almost unbearably touched. A lump formed in her throat when she looked at him standing there all rumpled and noble and earnest. And sexy as all get-out, but she pushed that particular observation to the back of her mind to concentrate on the conversation.

She rested a hand lightly on his arm and spoke in a voice that wasn't entirely steady. "That's very sweet of you, Cole, but you understand pregnant women don't have to get married these days, right?"

He covered her hand with his own. "Yes, I know. But you have to admit it would be much easier if you have someone to share the responsibilities. I like kids. Always thought I'd have at least one of my own someday, but I'd sort of given up on that expectation. I wasn't sure I'd ever marry again. I liked being married, but I get frazzled just thinking about the pressures and social expectations of courtship. Yet I can picture myself raising this child with you."

She drew her hand slowly from beneath his to latch on to a lock of her hair, twisting it so tightly her fingertip went numb. Was this real? Cole wasn't one to play practical jokes. And even if he were, this would hardly be funny. "I'm not sure what to say."

Still standing close, he studied her gravely, as if trying to read her mind. She wished him luck with that. The way her head was spinning, even she couldn't make sense of her thoughts.

"I can tell you're surprised, and I understand. But think about it, Stevie. It makes perfect sense. We could have a good life together. With my telecommuting job, I could watch the baby while you're working. Your career is flexible enough that we could coordinate our schedules around my business trips. I make a good living, so between the two of us, the child would be well cared for. I'm good with kids—and you have to admit I build a really great snowman," he added with a disarmingly self-deprecating smile.

"Wow." She swallowed, then said again, "Wow! You're actually serious."

He nodded. "It's a good plan, right? Win-win. For me, for you—and for this baby."

Oh, that was hardly a fair argument, she thought with a hard swallow. She'd told him she wished she could give her child a devoted dad. And she could hardly imagine a more upstanding candidate for the position.

She became aware that the hand not tangled in her hair had gone subconsciously to her stomach. She was still having trouble believing this was an actual proposal of marriage, but still she had to ask, "You'd really have no objection to raising another man's child as your own?"

Cole looked genuinely startled by the question. As straightforward as ever, he replied, "I've never had a particular desire to see my own face in miniature. My childhood best friend was adopted, something he discussed openly. He was closer to his adoptive family than I was to my biological one."

Though she didn't know the details of his estrangement from his father, she couldn't imagine why anyone wouldn't be grateful to have a son like Cole.

"Kids don't need a certified pedigree to make them happy," he added, just a hint of uncharacteristic wistfulness in his voice now. "They need love. Encouragement. Unwavering support. I can offer all those things to this child we can welcome together. Let's face it, neither of us expected this development, but we're both in the right place at the right time to accept the challenge."

Something deep inside her tightened in response to his words. "You've really given this a lot of consideration, haven't you?"

He nodded. "I've been thinking about it for days. I had to consider all the ramifications before I came to you. I'd never make a commitment I wasn't prepared to honor completely and permanently. I'm absolutely sure about this."

It wasn't often that naturally talkative Stevie found herself without words, but Cole had managed to strike her speechless. She almost wondered if she were dreaming this entire conversation, drifting into foolish daydreams about what might have been…

Cole reached out to gently untangle her hand from her hair, then cradled both her hands in his. She wasn't sure if he'd practiced this proposal, but he spoke without hesitation, visibly sincere. "Marry me, Stevie. You said I'm one of your best friends. I feel the same about you. We mesh well together, have from the start. We can make this work. We can give this child the type of home and family you and I both wanted growing up. I'm not making a sacrifice or being unselfish in this offer. I want very much to be a dad to this kid. I think I'd make a good one."

She'd spent her whole life acting on impulse, following her heart, her hunches, her instincts. Every one of those usual prompts urged her now to accept Cole's offer on the spot. Still, she owed it to him, to herself, to her child to take time to consider before she leaped this time.

"Think about it," he urged, reading the emotions chasing themselves across her face. "I don't want to rush you into anything that doesn't feel right to you, and nothing has to change between us if you choose to decline my proposal. We can still be friends. I just want you to know that I'm here for you and the baby, and that I hope—"

"Yes."

So much for caution.

He went still, his head cocked to one side as he eyed her closely. "Yes?"

She felt her fingers tremble in his big strong hands. His grip tightened just enough to show her that he felt it, too. She freed her hands and stepped back to give herself a little distance, drawing herself up to her full height, such as it was. Her voice was satisfactorily steady when she demanded, "Do you promise you'll always be a caring, committed father to this child, no matter what happens?"

"You have my word," he answered without a hint of hesitation. "You both do."

If there was one thing she'd learned about Cole Mc-Kellar during the past year, it was that he was the most honest man she'd ever met. Bluntly so, at times, but that was only part of his unique charm.

"Then the answer is yes."

It wasn't the hearts-and-flowers-and-violins marriage proposal she'd vaguely imagined for herself in youthful, Hollywood-tinted fantasies, but look where those silly daydreams had led her, how many times they'd let her down. She was going to be a mother now, and it was time to put unrealistic expectations behind her.

If she made a list of all the attributes she'd want for her child's father, Cole would match nearly every item on the page. Maybe he wasn't the type to write love songs for her or shower her with grand, romantic gestures, but the men who had done those things in the past hadn't stayed around to deal with the everyday realities of life. He wasn't claiming a grand passion for her— perhaps his late wife would always hold that position in his heart—but she knew he was quite fond of her, and she didn't doubt that he respected her intelligence and admired her success in her business. That meant a great deal to her.

Other men had claimed to love her, but hadn't stayed around to make a life with her. Cole would be there, stable, dependable, practical. She needed to work on being more like him—starting now.

"Yes," she repeated, more firmly this time.

A smile spread across his face and she had to admit he looked pleased. If he had any doubts about this plan, it wasn't visible in his expression. As for herself, she was still nervous—oh, hell, she was scared to her toenails—but she'd made her decision. She gave her tummy a little pat, sending a silent message in that direction. *You're welcome, kid.*

"Great," he said with obvious satisfaction. "We'll make this work, Stevie, I promise."

"I believe you." She would certainly do her part, she vowed.

Her legs seemed to have weakened, so she moved to sit on the couch. Cole sat beside her, drawing his phone from his pocket. She frowned a little. Was he already calling someone with the news? Was he really this excited about—

But he'd merely opened his calendar. "So when do you want to do this? The baby is due in—six months, right?"

She nodded, trying to focus on practical details. "Yes."

"So that doesn't give us a lot of time to take care of things. We'll have to decide where to live, set up a nursery, work out our schedules, that sort of thing. You, um—do you want a big wedding? Because if you do—"

"No," she assured him quickly. "I'd prefer something small and simple."

She could see relief cross his face, though knowing Cole, she suspected he'd have agreed to a huge affair if she'd said she wanted one.

"I don't need my parents there," he said. "Considering they don't even like being in the same state at the same time, they'd hardly want to attend the same wedding. They'll probably be relieved they don't have to make the effort. I'm pretty sure my mom will be pleased at the prospect of having a grandchild. I think she'd pretty much given up on the idea."

She twisted her fingers in her lap. Would his mother really welcome this child, even though her son wasn't the biological father? "Are you, um, going to tell your parents that I was already pregnant when you and I decided to get married?"

Cole shrugged. "As far as I'm concerned, it's unnecessary. I won't lie, but there's no need to tell everyone our business. You can make the decision with your mother and brother. We'll tell the child when he or she is old enough to understand, of course, and I guess your closest friends will know the truth, but I'd be fine with letting the rest make their own assumptions."

"That works for me, too," she murmured.

He nodded, putting that item behind them before returning to the previous one. "What about you? Do you want to wait until your mother and brother can get here to have the ceremony?"

She barely had to think about it before shaking her head. "Mom isn't really interested in ceremonies—and she's never been a big fan of marriage," she added with a wry laugh. "She'll be satisfied with hearing the details afterward and then flying in for a visit after the baby arrives. Same goes for my brother."

"And what about your friends?"

"Jenny and Tess are going to be…surprised." Which was the understatement of the year, of course.

Cole studied her expression. "How do you think they'll feel about our plans?"

"I don't know," she admitted.

She was sure her friends would be concerned she was acting on impulse and would urge her to take more time to think about all of this, despite the pregnancy deadline. Bonded with their soul mates, they would obviously want the same for her. Jenny had turned down a socially advantageous proposal from a wealthy and connected attorney to wed the cop she'd loved since their college years. Tess's engagement to her employer might have started out as an arrangement meant to assuage their matchmaking relatives during the holidays, but it hadn't taken them long to realize they'd been deeply in love for some time.

Both Jenny and Tess would certainly remind Stevie that she had always been the one to defend the fairy tale version of romance, to insist marriage should be based on passion, not practicality. But their circumstances were very different from her own, she reminded herself. They'd had only their own best interests to consider during their courtships. Jenny understood the pain of growing up without a father, her own having died before she was even born, but would she approve of Stevie's decision to provide for her baby's needs over her own silly fantasies?

"I don't know," she repeated.

"Would you change your mind if they do disapprove?"

She shook her head firmly. "Of course not. It's just that I'm not quite sure how to explain it to them. As I've said, I haven't even told them yet that I'm pregnant. I just don't want them to worry about me."

As much as she hated to admit it, things were changing between her and her friends with marriages and babies coming into the picture. It was inevitable, she supposed. They would always be close, but the time they could spend together would be even more limited with these new responsibilities.

"Here's an idea." Cole drummed the fingers of one hand lightly against his thigh. She could tell by his expression that he'd turned his full attention to solving her latest dilemma. "Instead of telling them ahead of time and dealing with their questions and opinions, why don't you just present it to them as a fait accompli? We could elope, then tell them we're married and we're committed to raising this child together. There would be little they could say at that point except to congratulate you and wish you well."

She blinked. "Not tell them beforehand? But Jen and I have always told each other everything. Tess, too, since we met her."

"You haven't told them you're pregnant."

She winced in response to that very reasonable rebuttal. "No."

"What's your schedule tomorrow?" he asked after a moment.

The seemingly abrupt change of subject made her blink again before answering, "I have a meeting in the morning, but it should only take a couple of hours."

"Can you be done by noon? I have a few things to deal with, but I can be finished by lunchtime. There's no waiting period to be married in this state, so we could leave at around one o'clock tomorrow afternoon, pick up a marriage license and stop at one of those little wedding chapels in the Ozarks. Afterward, we'll drive into Missouri and spend a couple nights at a nice inn in Branson, and be back at work Monday morning. I wish I could take you somewhere special for a real honeymoon, but my schedule is pretty tight at the moment and I'm sure yours is, too, getting ready for your maternity leave and all."

"Tomorrow," she repeated somewhat blankly, feeling swept along by a current that had surged out of control. She'd already agreed to marry him, so why did setting a time cause a flicker of panic inside her? "You're talking about getting married tomorrow?"

"Well, we could wait a little longer if you need more time."

"I—" She chewed her lower lip as she considered. Though she felt a bit cowardly to admit it, she could see the appeal of telling her friends after the fact rather than facing a barrage of questions and doubts and advice. Cole was right—this way it would be too late for them to try to talk her out of marrying him. Too late to talk herself out of it. "Tomorrow works for me."

He gave her knee a little squeeze, his fingers lingering long enough to make her vividly aware of his touch. "I'll make the arrangements with the chapel and a hotel. February is hardly peak tourist season, so we shouldn't have trouble getting reservations. Some of the Branson theaters are probably closed for the season, but I'm sure a few are still open. It'll be fun, right?"

"Fun." Stevie laughed in bemusement and pressed her cold hands to her warm cheeks. "How is it that you can make even the craziest plan sound absolutely rational?"

Cole had the grace to smile crookedly as he rose from the couch. "My special talent?"

"Apparently."

"Well?"

Rising as he did, she drew a slightly shaky breath and pressed a hand to her stomach. "Okay. I have a consultation at nine in the morning, but I can be ready to leave by one o'clock."

As matter-of-fact as Cole was being about all this, she wouldn't have been entirely surprised if he'd sealed the deal by offering his hand to shake. Instead, he reached into his pocket. For the first time since he'd blindsided her with this plan he'd obviously considered so carefully, she saw a hint of uncertainty in his expression. "I picked up something for you while I was in Chicago. I hope you like it."

"I'm sure I'll—" Her voice faded when she saw the little velvet box resting on his palm. "Oh."

"I wanted to be prepared in case you said yes." He opened the hinged lid to reveal the contents.

Her breath caught when the overhead light glittered off a diamond set on a white gold band. It was exactly the type of ring she'd have expected Cole to choose, simple and classic. Even the choice of square-cut over the slightly more traditional round stone was typical of him—though the gesture itself was certainly unexpected.

"It's beautiful, Cole." Her voice sounded husky to her own ears.

He caught her hand and slid the ring on her finger. She told herself it was a good omen that it fit surprisingly well. Her hands were small, but the ring wasn't overpowering. In fact, she'd have said it was exactly right for her.

He was watching her face. "If you'd prefer another style, we can swap it for—"

She curled her fingers protectively around the ring. "This one is perfect."

"I'm glad you like it. So, I'll go now and start making arrangements. This time tomorrow, we'll be in Branson."

And married, she added silently, swallowing hard.

She could tell his mind was already engaged with lists of tasks he wanted to complete before tomorrow. She knew how he got when he was focused on a deadline. He was probably itching to tap away at his trustworthy little tablet. "All right. See you tomorrow."

She walked him to the door, feeling as if she were moving in an odd sort of slow motion. She'd begun the day as an anxious, single mother-to-be. Only a few hours later, she found herself engaged to be married to a man who was busily planning their future while she still reeled from his proposal.

He let himself out, closing the door behind him. With a little sigh, Stevie started to turn away. She paused with a start when the door swept open again. Cole stepped back inside, his expression rueful.

"That was a lousy way to conclude our conversation, wasn't it?" he asked. "I think I can do much better."

Before she quite realized his intention, he gathered her into his arms and pressed his lips to hers.

As first kisses went, especially with such little fanfare, this one was impressive. Solid and sturdy, Cole enveloped her, engulfed her. Every feminine nerve ending inside her responded to that potent masculinity with a rush of sensation unlike anything she'd experienced before.

She was kissing Cole! Or he was kissing her. And if ever she had contemplated what it might be like to do so—and she'd imagined it on more than a few occasions, just for curiosity—the reality was more explosive than she could ever have predicted. How could she possibly have suspected that the quiet numbers cruncher next door kissed like a dashing pirate?

His lips were firm, warm, skilled. The hint of his late-day beard was pleasantly rough against her softer skin. He tasted of sexy, spicy, virile male; a potent combination that made her suddenly, unexpectedly hungry for more. She couldn't quite hold back the tiny murmur of protest when he drew his mouth a couple inches from hers, breaking the contact.

Cole looked almost as dazed as she felt when their gazes locked. And then he swooped in for another taste, and she discovered to her amazement that the first kiss hadn't been a fluke. She couldn't have said how long it lasted, or which of them moved closer to deepen the kiss, to press their bodies together. She couldn't help noticing that Cole was tautly aroused as he thrust his tongue between her parted lips for a more thorough exploration.

How long had this embrace been building? Hours? Days? Months? Was it possible she wasn't the only one who'd wondered what it would be like, who'd secretly wished to find out?

She didn't realize she was gripping his shirt in both white-knuckled fists until he finally, firmly set her back a step, carefully untangling her fingers from the now-wrinkled fabric. Wow. Did she say that aloud or was the word just echoing in her otherwise blank mind?

His face a bit flushed, Cole shifted his weight uncomfortably, then cleared his throat before saying, "Well. That was…reassuring."

She blinked, not entirely sure how to respond to that comment. It wasn't the adjective she'd have chosen to describe the embrace. Amazing, maybe. Spectacular. Toe-curlingly stimulating, even. But…reassuring?

After only a moment, Cole chuckled huskily, gave her shoulder a little squeeze, then opened the door. "I'll call you later. If you need anything in the meantime, you know where to find me."

The door closed behind him again and this time it stayed shut. Stevie stood without moving for what seemed like a very long time. In a daze, she pushed her hair from her overwarm face.

As she turned slowly back into her living room, she felt as if she should pinch herself to make sure she was really awake. Either this was one truly bizarre dream, or she'd just agreed to marry her next-door neighbor. Tomorrow!

Stevie could usually pack for a week in a carry-on bag, and rarely spent more than a few minutes deciding what to take. Yet it took her more than an hour to choose and pack the next day. And all for a two-night trip, she thought with a shake of her head as she stood in the middle of her bedroom, dithering over shoe choices.

It wasn't as if she needed anything different from her usual informal, somewhat bohemian wardrobe, not in Branson. With its live theaters, shopping malls, themed restaurants, golf courses and arcades, the town nestled in the Ozarks on the banks of sprawling Lake Taneycomo was a cheerfully cheesy tourist magnet.

There hadn't been a lot of extra money for vacations and travel when she'd been a child, but two or three times each year she and her mother and brother had made the just-over-three-hour road trip to Branson for a relatively inexpensive family weekend. She still had warm memories from those trips, which she'd mentioned to Cole during a couple of their rambling, lengthy chats. Did he remember? Probably. Cole didn't forget much.

She zipped her suitcase, then frowned at it, wondering if she'd packed enough. No. She wasn't going to second-guess this. It was only a weekend trip.

It was also her honeymoon, she thought, chewing on her lower lip as she gazed down at her ring. This wasn't at all what she'd imagined when she'd ever fantasized about a honeymoon.

Was she dressed appropriately for an elopement? Had the weather been warmer, she'd have worn something sleeveless and lacy, perhaps. There was no snow on the ground now, but it was cold enough that she'd have shivered in lace. She'd chosen, instead, a dusky blue sweater dress with black leggings and tall boots. The dress had come from Jenny's shop, and Jenny had told her the color made her eyes look brighter and bluer. Sometimes she wore a wide belt with it, but she left off the belt this time, accessorizing with a chunky ebony-bead necklace, instead.

Posing in front of the mirror, she looked hard at her midsection. She still doubted anyone could tell her condition just by looking at her. Had she not seen the positive pregnancy test and heard the doctor's confirmation, she would hardly believe it herself. It still didn't seem quite real. Nor did the fact that she was going to be a married woman in a few hours.

She opened the silver jewelry box on her dresser to take out the hoop earrings she planned to wear today. As she removed them, a narrow slip of paper caught her attention. She'd saved it from a fortune cookie; she didn't even remember exactly when, but she'd had it for several years. Something about its message had spoken to her: *You will live an unexpected life*.

She laughed shortly. "You surely got that right, Confucius."

Cole was pleased that they were in the car and on the road exactly on the schedule they'd agreed upon. Though he and Stevie hadn't confided the reason they'd both be out of town for the next two nights, they'd arranged for Lori to check on Dusty tomorrow, so the long weekend was all cleared for their brief honeymoon. Even the weather was cooperating. It was cold, but the roads were dry and the sky a cloudless pale blue. He took that as a good sign.

He was very much aware of how close they sat in the front seats of his SUV. He could reach easily enough across the narrow console to take her hand or rest his on her knee. Because that thought was all too tempting, he tightened his fingers on the steering wheel and tried not to think about the kisses that had left him tossing and turning in his bed most of the night.

He didn't have to worry about awkward silences during the drive. Though he'd seen the self-consciousness in her eyes when she'd answered the door, Stevie wasn't the type to be quiet when she was flustered. Just the opposite, actually; she tended to babble. Cole wasn't sure she took a breath during the first hour of their drive. She chattered about so many random topics he couldn't even keep up, her hands fluttering around her like restless little birds.

Though he didn't say much in return—couldn't have slipped in more than a word or two if he'd wanted to— he didn't mind her frenetic monologue. Nor did he try to calm her. She had every reason to be jittery. He was a little nervous, himself—not because he had doubts about the plans they'd made, but because he hoped he was up to the massive responsibilities he was taking on. He had to admit he'd assigned himself a daunting task. Torn between bittersweet memories of the past, concerns for the future and frustrated physical desire, he hadn't gotten much sleep last night.

"Oh, my gosh." Stevie covered her cheeks with her hands, laughing ruefully. "I'm talking a thousand miles a minute, aren't I? I haven't given you a chance to speak at all. Sorry."

"No need to apologize. I enjoy listening to you. It makes the drive go by faster."

"Yes, well, I've run out of small talk."

"Maybe we should discuss some of the decisions we have ahead of us. I made a list last night..."

She chuckled softly. "Of course you did. Should I pull out your trusty notebook?"

He didn't mind her teasing any more than her chattering. It was all just part of what made up Stevie, and he couldn't imagine why anyone would want to change her.

"There's no need," he said with his own attempt at levity. "I memorized the list."

It pleased him that she laughed before asking, "Okay, what's the first item on the agenda?"

He started with an easy question. "How are you feeling? Still no morning sickness?"

"Not a day. Unlike poor Jenny. She said she starting getting sick almost immediately. She didn't tell us about the pregnancy until Wednesday because she said she was afraid she'd jinx it, but she's been dealing with morning sickness for a couple of weeks."

"You're lucky, then."

"I suppose." As if hearing how the words might have sounded, she shook her head quickly. "It's not that I want to be sick, of course. I just don't really feel pregnant, you know? I've seen the tests and I saw an ultrasound and heard the heartbeat at this week's doctor's appointment, but sometimes it still just doesn't feel real."

"I can imagine. Well, not really, because it's not something I'll ever experience, obviously, but it must be an odd sensation. You said you saw an ultrasound?"

"Yes. I have the printout at home. It's pretty cool. Still just a little peanut a couple inches long, which I guess is why I'm not really showing yet, but you can see the little arms and legs and some facial features."

Another ripple of nerves coursed through him at the thought of actually seeing the baby he planned to raise as his own. "Can you tell yet if it's a boy or a girl?" Not that it mattered to him.

"No, not yet. I'll have another ultrasound after twenty weeks and we should be able to tell then."

"Will you want to know then or would you rather be surprised at delivery?"

She laughed wryly. "I wouldn't be patient enough to wait that long. It'll be hard enough waiting until the ultrasound to find out."

Exactly as he'd have expected from her. And, being the type who always liked to be prepared, he felt the same way. "Have you bought any baby supplies yet?"

"Nothing yet. Except…"

"Except?"

"I bought a night-light shaped like a turtle. It's made to sit on a table beside the crib. The shell glows and there's a battery backup that keeps it illuminated even if the power goes out. I was afraid of the dark when I was little, and I thought maybe the baby will be, too."

Curious, he slanted her a sideways glance. "Are you still afraid of the dark?"

"Sometimes," she admitted. "I still sleep with a flashlight close at hand."

That surprised him. He hadn't thought Stevie was afraid of anything. "Is there a particular reason you're afraid of the dark?"

She hesitated a minute, then sighed. "I've always had that tendency, but it got worse when I was nine and Tom was ten and a half. I had a night-light in my room, but I still got scared when I heard funny noises. I didn't say much about it because Tom made fun of me, and you know how siblings can be."

"I was an only child, but I saw enough of my friends' siblings to get the picture."

"Anyway, Mom had taken a part-time second job working at a hotel desk in the evenings, earning extra money for Tom to get braces. Mrs. Clausen from next door came over to stay with us on those evenings. One night there was a thunderstorm and the power went out. I woke up in a totally dark room and got scared. I called and called, but no one answered and I was certain I was alone in the house—well, except for maybe the monsters under the bed or in the closet," she added ruefully.

"Where was Mrs. Clausen?" he asked, caught up in the story.

Stevie gave a low laugh that held little humor. "Stuck in the front bathroom. She got flustered in the dark and couldn't find the door lock. It was probably no more than minutes before she managed to get to me, but it seemed like hours. I was sobbing hysterically by the time she made her way to me."

"And your brother?"

"Slept through the whole storm."

"I'm sure you were frightened. That must have been traumatic for you."

Her hands fluttered again. "I grew up. Got over it to an extent. I still keep a flashlight on the nightstand, but I'm pretty confident now that there are no monsters under the bed or in the closet."

"Thank you for sharing that with me. I know it must be a painful memory but it means a lot that you trust me with it."

She reached over to pat his thigh, her soft laugh more natural this time. "It was just an anecdote, Cole, not a confession to my priest."

Reaction to that familiar touch surged through him, but he pushed it away. She had a way of gently poking at him when he got too formal and serious. He covered her hand with his and squeezed before gripping the steering wheel again, silently acknowledging he'd gotten the message. Still, he'd meant every word. If he and Stevie were going to make this work, they had to be honest and open with each other.

Stevie drew her hand away and laced her fingers in her lap. Her voice sounded a bit higher-pitched when she said, "Anyway, Mom stopped working nights after that incident. She bought Tom's braces on a payment plan. Fortunately my teeth were straight."

He laughed, then asked, "How do you think your mom will feel about becoming a grandmother?"

"She most definitely won't be a traditional grandma. She'll wonder why we're bothering with what she calls 'the obsolete and unnecessary institution of marriage.' I'm sure she'll come see the baby as soon as she can make arrangements. We gathered in Tennessee at my brother's house for Christmas, but I didn't know about the pregnancy then—or hadn't accepted the possibility yet."

"I'll bring her here for your due date, if she'd like to be here. You should have your mother with you."

"That's sweet of you, but I'll buy her ticket. I do okay financially, you know. Well enough to live comfortably, if not extravagantly. As I told you, I'm budgeting for my leave time, so…"

Her voice drifted off with another vague gesture of her hands. A very self-sufficient woman, his wife-to-be. That was only one of the many things he admired about her, though he still hoped she'd let him help her out.

He slanted a sideways glance at her. She looked very pretty today. That blue dress was especially flattering with her blond hair and big blue eyes. The soft knit fabric hugged her curves—and for such a petite woman, she had very nice curves. He cleared his throat, shifted in his seat, and tightened his grip on the steering wheel.

"I want to buy the kid a stuffed tiger," he said to distract himself. "Maybe we'll find one this weekend."

"A tiger?" Stevie twisted in her seat to look at him.

He nodded. "You had a night-light, I had Stripy. My uncle Bob—my dad's younger brother—gave him to me when I was four, maybe five. My parents were fighting then, splitting up and getting back together, shuttling me between them and my paternal grandparents. I never knew where I'd be spending the next night or whether my parents would be too quiet or yelling at each other. I started having nightmares, waking up screaming nearly every night. Uncle Bob bought me the tiger to chase away the monsters at night. He was a big *Calvin and Hobbes* fan. He'd read the comic strips to me from the newspaper."

"The tiger stopped your nightmares?"

He shrugged. "Didn't stop them. But when I woke up, Stripy was always there, and it made me feel better. The nightmares stopped after my parents split up for good and we all settled into new, more peaceful routines. I spent most of my childhood on my grandparents' cattle farm in El Paso, Arkansas, while Mom went back to college. Dad poured his energy into building his car repair business. With the exception of a couple of rocky years, I had a pretty good childhood. But I still have fond memories of Stripy. I think our kid should have one, though I can promise you we'll never put him—or her—through what my folks did to me. They got married too young, had a baby before they knew what they wanted for themselves. You and I are old enough and realistic enough to avoid all that foolishness."

"Absolutely," she said with almost grim determination. "We'll give him—or her—a stable, safe and secure childhood so he—or she—never has to depend on a night-light or a stuffed toy to chase away the monsters under the bed."

He frowned for a moment at the road ahead, processing her words as he drove in silence. He knew, of course, that she'd accepted his unexpected proposal for the benefit of her baby, just as the child's best interests had been a strong consideration for him when he'd offered. But he hoped she didn't see their marriage as a sacrifice on her part. "I want you to be happy, too, Stevie. We'll have a good life together. I'll always be there for you when you need support or encouragement."

She patted his thigh again, a vaguely unsatisfying gesture this time as it seemed entirely too indulgent. "And when you come back from those dull business trips, Dusty and Li'l Peanut and I will be there to welcome you with hugs and a home-cooked meal."

"Sounds great," he said, and meant it. It sounded ideal. He should stop trying to second-guess her thoughts and feelings—he wasn't good at it, anyway—and just accept his good fortune.

He pushed thoughts of the past away and focused instead on the future. After all, this was the beginning of their life together. He would be spending the weekend with this fascinating, desirable woman...and he planned to make this honeymoon a memory Stevie would always cherish.

Chapter Four

Cole really was an organizational genius, Stevie concluded an hour later. He'd taken care of logistical details for their elopement that hadn't even yet occurred to her, including the marriage license they dealt with immediately upon their arrival at their wedding destination.

She saw him caught off guard only once during those preparations.

"Stephanie?" he asked in surprise when they'd filled out their license application. "Your full name is Stephanie Joan McLane?"

She wrinkled her nose as she nodded. "Mom named me after Stevie Nicks—whose birth name was Stephanie—and Joan Jett, her two favorite women singers. My brother is Thomas Neil, after Tom Petty and Neil Young. He's always said it was a good thing Mom wasn't a country music fan or we might have ended up answering to Dolly and Porter."

That had made Cole laugh. He had such a rich, deep laugh. She hoped to hear it often during their upcoming years together, she thought wistfully.

The little wedding chapel he'd reserved was close to the state border, only some forty miles from their honeymoon destination of Branson, Missouri. Located in an old, white-frame church with battered but gleaming wood floors and rows of antique oak pews, it was generously, almost overly, decorated with white silk flowers and big red hearts. Romantic instrumental music played from speakers. A portly, sixtysomething officiate with a beatific smile and twinkling eyes welcomed them warmly, introducing himself as Pastor Dave and his equally plump and smiling wife, Luanne.

"You were very lucky we had this slot available today. Valentine's Day is our most popular day for elopements, you know," he confided, pumping Cole's hand and winking at Stevie. "Got five more weddings scheduled before the day's done."

Valentine's Day. Stevie just barely stopped herself from slapping her hands to her cheeks with a gasp. How flustered had she been today that she'd written the date probably half a dozen times without considering the significance? She'd been vaguely aware that the holiday was upon them, of course, but she hadn't watched much TV or spent much time on social media during the past few busy, emotionally stressful weeks. How on earth *had* Cole managed to make wedding and honeymoon reservations in less than twenty-four hours for this particular weekend? He'd assured her they would be staying at a very nice hotel and even had tickets to a couple of popular shows.

Watching him slip a couple of bills to their beaming host, she suspected he'd quietly greased a few palms.

And he'd done this all for her. She bit her lower lip, then released it immediately to keep from chewing off her freshly applied gloss. She wanted to look nice in the Elite Matrimonial Photo Package Luanne would take with her digital camera.

"Shall we begin?" Pastor Dave waved a hand toward the altar at the front of the little chapel, looking surreptitiously at the antique clock on the wall behind him as he turned. "You requested the nondenominational religious ceremony, is that correct, Mr. McKellar?"

"Yes," Cole agreed, glancing at Stevie as if for confirmation.

She managed a smile and a nod, resisting an impulse to nervously twist her hair. *No second thoughts*, she ordered herself. *For once in your life, you're doing the sensible thing.*

"Here you go, Miss McLane." Luanne pressed three long-stemmed red roses tied together with a white satin ribbon in Stevie's hand, then stepped back to raise her camera. "Give us a big smile, hon."

The roses were pretty, part of the Special Deluxe Elopement Package. Holding them gently in her left hand, Stevie set her small handbag on a front pew, rummaged in it for a moment, then turned toward her groom. "I'm ready."

"When I heard your fine Scottish surnames, I chose a special wedding song just for the two of you," Pastor Dave confided as he moved to the small lectern at the front of the room. He pressed a couple of buttons and after a brief pause, a bagpipe version of *Ode to Joy* poured from the overhead speakers. Stevie slanted a glance at Cole to find him smiling down at her in a way that almost elicited a completely inappropriate giggle. She heard the click-click of Luanne's camera as Pastor

Dave began his simple ceremony, barely referring to the little book in his hands as he recited words he must have intoned countless times before.

Somehow she managed to pay attention, and to respond appropriately at the correct times. She smiled faintly when the officiate read her almost-husband's full name. Cole Douglas McKellar. A fine Scottish name, indeed.

She moistened her lips as Cole's gaze locked with hers. A ripple of awareness coursed through her at the thought that this attractive, caring and complex man would now be bound to her. They would share a home, a future. A bed. As hectic as the past twenty-four hours had been, she'd hardly had time to even think about that part of their marriage. She realized suddenly that she was looking forward to the journey they'd embarked on together that morning.

What was Cole thinking? Feeling? He looked as at ease as ever. But on closer inspection, was there just a hint of tension in his dark eyes? She had no doubt he was taking these vows very seriously, but was he wondering whether he'd acted on an uncharacteristic and perhaps imprudent impulse? Was he having second thoughts?

Pastor Dave peered at them over the top of his reading glasses. "Do y'all have rings?"

"I do." Cole drew a white gold band from the pocket of the charcoal sport coat he wore with a pale blue shirt, lighter gray pants and a blue and gray patterned tie. Knowing how much he hated wearing ties, she was touched that he'd gone to the effort of dressing up for this occasion, even though they had no audience for their ceremony other than Pastor Dave and Luanne.

"I have one, too," she said, opening her left hand to

reveal the band she'd taken from her purse. Like hers, it was white gold, his with a brushed finish. She'd bought it that very morning. She'd stopped into a jewelry store in the same business center as her office and taken only a few minutes to select a ring that seemed to suit Cole's tastes, making a guess at his size. She saw surprise flit fleetingly across his face. Had he thought she'd forgotten to get a ring? Or had he never actually expected to wear a wedding band again?

And here she was, second-guessing his emotions again. She shook her head slightly and slipped the ring on his finger when prompted by Pastor Dave. It fit well enough, not snug but not so loose it would slip off. She saw Cole look down at his hand as if to admire the band there, and she hoped that was a sign that he liked it.

Luanne moved into position behind Pastor Dave with her camera raised as he pronounced them husband and wife. The camera snapped noisily when he added, "Y'all can seal this deal with a kiss now."

Stevie's giggle was smothered beneath Cole's willingly cooperative lips. And while the presence of their approving audience held the kiss in check, she was vividly reminded of the more heated kisses they'd exchanged in private yesterday.

Her heart tripped in her chest. She and Cole would be spending this night together as husband and wife. Judging by the fireworks that went off inside her whenever their lips met, this was going to be a very special honeymoon, indeed!

Cole had made a reservation at a nice hotel just off Branson's main thoroughfare. Stevie's palms felt damp as she followed him into the elevator for the ninth floor. Apparently she'd been so focused on the impromptu wedding that she hadn't looked much farther ahead. She certainly hadn't anticipated how nervous she would be at the prospect of officially beginning their honeymoon! Nervous—but excited, she realized with a flutter of anticipation.

Cole swiped the key card without looking around at her, then moved out of the way to allow her to precede him into the room. *Suite*, she corrected herself when she walked in and looked around. In addition to a king-sized bed and a small table with two chairs, there was a pretty little sitting area with what she assumed to be a sleeper sofa and an armchair. Her attention was drawn almost immediately back to that huge bed. She hoped Cole didn't hear her hard swallow.

Cole set down their bags before turning to her. Though she couldn't stop glancing toward the bed, he seemed to be making an effort to avoid looking at it. "Would you like to change before dinner, or are you good in what you're wearing?" he asked.

"This is fine, thanks."

"You don't mind if I get rid of this tie, do you?" He was already tugging at the knot.

She smiled. "I'm surprised you kept it on this long. By all means, make yourself comfortable. It's not like ties are the typical dress code for Branson."

He shed both jacket and tie and pulled a navy V-neck sweater from his bag to tug over his pale blue shirt. "That's better," he said with a sigh of such relief that she had to laugh.

She reached up to smooth his hair, resisting an urge to play in it for a bit. She really did love his springy dark hair.

Aware again of that big bed behind her, she dropped her hand and took a step back. "So. Dinner?"

Was his smile just a bit strained when he nodded? "Dinner," he said, and motioned toward the door.

Carrying a plastic mug shaped like a cowboy boot, Stevie reentered the hotel room later that evening with a slightly weary sigh. It had been a long, momentous day after an early start, and she was tired, but not in a bad way. On a whim, she retrieved the three red roses she'd stuck into a glass of water earlier and transferred them to the souvenir boot mug. The blooms were already starting to wilt, but she set them prominently in the center of the table, stepping back to admire them while Cole hung up their coats.

He turned to study her makeshift centerpiece, then pushed a hand through his hair, speaking wryly. "So, your wedding night festivities consisted of sitting on benches in an arena, eating pork and chicken and corn on the cob with our hands, while entertainers did tricks on horseback for the dinner show."

She giggled. He was not exaggerating. "Maybe the place didn't offer silverware, but the food was delicious and the show was fun."

Cole looked as though he tried to smile in response, but he wasn't very successful at it. Taking a step toward her, he placed his hands on her shoulders and gazed down at her gravely. "I feel as though I should apologize."

She felt her eyebrows rise. "For...?"

"I doubt very much that this was the wedding experience of your dreams. A one-day engagement. Pastor Dave and Luanne. Two nights in a town that's basically one big amusement park. A wedding night barbecue dinner shared at a long table with a group of senior citizens who came from Wisconsin on a tour bus. Not exactly a tropical resort or a European villa."

"I happened to enjoy that dinner," she assured him, letting her hands rest on his chest. "And the sweet little old man sitting at my other side kept me laughing all through the meal and the show. It was a pleasure to share a bench with him."

"He was flirting with you."

"Yes, he was. He said he's ninety, but he still has an eye for the ladies. He asked me to run away with him after dessert. I told him I would have, but I'm a married woman now."

She felt Cole's fingers flex on her shoulders in response to those words, perhaps a subconscious reaction. Probably he was still adjusting to the reality of being a married man again after so many years of bachelorhood. That was certainly understandable.

"I'm glad you didn't run off with the old guy," he said, a slight smile now softening his troubled expression.

Aware of how closely they were standing, she moistened her lips. It would require only a slight shift of her weight and she could be in his arms, cradled against that warm, strong chest. She shifted her hands a bit, savoring the feel of firm muscles beneath his soft sweater. Her shiny new rings glinted on her left ring finger. "So am I."

His gaze lowered, and if she wasn't mistaken he focused intently on her mouth. What was he thinking? she wondered. Before she could ask, he blinked, and the moment was over. He glanced at the bed, and those brown eyes darkened. Frowning, he turned his head to look at the sofa bed in the sitting area. "It's been an eventful day. I'm sure you're tired. You can take the big bed. I can sleep on the sofa bed."

"Cole." She tightened her grip on his sweater as she interrupted. It was apparent that he was trying so hard to keep his tone casual and considerate, careful not to cause her any discomfort or embarrassment on their wedding night. Nerves danced frantically beneath her skin, but she held his gaze steadily. "First, you need to understand that you don't owe me apologies for today. We had a lovely wedding. The dinner show made me laugh, which I always appreciate. I expect to have a fun weekend with you here in a place that holds many happy childhood memories for me. It doesn't take a tropical resort or a European villa to make me happy."

He cupped her cheek with one hand. "Maybe you don't need them, but you deserve them. I'd like to take you to both someday. In the meantime, if there's anything special you want to do while we're here this weekend, just let me know."

He was trying so hard to please her. Very sweet, but unnecessary. She wasn't that high maintenance.

Her hands still clutching his soft sweater, she rose slowly on tiptoes, trying to read his expression as she brought her mouth close to his. Did he truly want to spend their wedding night on the sofa bed? Perhaps they'd entered a marriage of convenience based on building a stable family for this child and for themselves—but he needed to know she considered it a real marriage. She didn't think either of them would be satisfied for long being nothing more than friendly roommates. She knew she wouldn't.

Now that she'd allowed herself to acknowledge her attraction to him, just standing this close to him made her skin tingle, her pulse accelerate. And from the way his eyes darkened as she moved closer to him, it was clear he had healthy desires of his own. Though he'd kept his private life to himself for the most part, and rarely confided details of where he went on his nights out with friends, she'd never thought of her quiet neighbor as monk-like.

"Thank you for taking care of everything this weekend for us, Cole," she murmured against his lips. "You've done a wonderful job."

She kissed him before he could respond.

Fueled by simmering emotions, by nerves and uncertainties, hopes and resolve, the kiss was spectacular. Stevie threw herself into it, pushing away thoughts and doubts in favor of feelings and sensations.

When she pressed her abdomen to the gratifyingly hard ridge in his pants, he froze, then broke off the kiss as if he'd abruptly come to his senses. "I, uh…"

He cleared his throat, hard, his hands on her shoulders. To keep her close? Or to hold her away? He looked as though even he wasn't quite sure of his intentions.

"Look, Stevie, I know I rushed us into all of this. I mean, I tend not to waste much time when I get a good idea, but now that we've taken care of the formalities, there's certainly no pressure for you to…we have the rest of our lives to…I mean, just so you know, when the time is right, I'm here for you, but—"

"Cole," she said again, reaching up to lay her fingers against his clever mouth. It was so rare to see him flustered and babbling. She couldn't help being both amused and charmed. "We're married. We made promises to each other in that chapel today in front of Pastor Dave and Luanne. I want to share a bed with my husband, if he's interested."

"I'm interested." Cole's voice was husky. "Been interested for longer than I've wanted to admit."

A part of her had known, she thought as she took his hand. Just because they hadn't acknowledged the attraction didn't mean it hadn't always been there.

She took his hand and moved a step backward toward the big bed. Looking up at him through her lashes, she smiled. "I'm very happy to hear that."

She was already tugging at the hem of his sweater. Judging from touch alone, those clothes hid a seriously fine body. Plus, there'd been that brief glimpse of a chiseled chest the day he'd changed the light bulb. Now she was eager to explore it more closely. His hands joined hers where she worked at the buttons of his shirt, and she left him to finish while she shed her boots.

They tossed their clothes aside quickly as impatience took over. But she had the presence of mind to glimpse at his body as he revealed it. She took in the strong planes of his back and chest and the rock-hard muscles of his thighs. He stopped at a pair of boxers, and she was denied the full view she anticipated. Before she could remove her underwear he stepped forward and took her in his arms, tumbling her onto the pillows, his mouth on hers as their limbs tangled. He was so warm. Solid. Being in his arms was like being wrapped in armor. She felt safe. Protected. It was a novel feeling for someone who'd spent her whole life taking care of herself and taking care of others. Quite a seductive sensation in itself—not to mention how very good he felt on top of her.

For a man who spent so much time working on computers, Cole McKellar kept himself in excellent physical condition. And he proved very quickly that he knew exactly what to do with that great body.

It was no surprise to her at all that he was a thorough and unselfish lover, two adjectives that seemed the perfect description of the man she'd come to know during the past year. Now that they were in the bed, he took his time, lingering and savoring as he explored, caressed, tantalized, then unhurriedly moved on. He was so gentle at first, so obviously intent not to cause her discomfort. She was the one who lost patience, growling beneath her breath and tugging at him until he got the message with a low, willing laugh.

He stripped her bra, his hands moving more eagerly, less carefully now over her breasts as he revealed them. Then he slowly, excruciatingly slowly, slipped off her panties, dragging his fingers down her legs as he pulled them off. When he returned to hover over her, she wasted no more time. To convince him she was neither fragile nor shy, she matched his kiss hungrily, letting her tongue tangle with his. She slipped one leg around him and in one smooth motion his body merged with hers. Her breath escaped in a gasp of pleasure, echoed by Cole's deep groan. He brought her other leg around him and went even deeper, and she welcomed him into her. Moving with him in an age-old rhythm, she built inexorably toward a powerful climax, one so intense that she could not think or speak or even moan. Just feel.

He followed her immediately, and from the contented groan he gave right before his release, she reasoned he felt the same.

"Happy Valentine's Day, Stevie," she heard him murmur some time later, after he'd recovered enough breath to speak. Not quite to the point of speech, herself, she merely smiled sleepily and nestled contentedly into his bare shoulder.

Cole lay awake for some time after Stevie slept. He hadn't yet turned off the small lamp in the sitting area, and there was just enough light in the room for him to see her sprawled bonelessly beside him in the big bed, clutching her pillow into a ball with both arms. Her blond curls tumbled riotously around her shoulders, partially hiding her face, though he could see that her lips were parted in what he thought looked like a soft little smile. She looked sated and utterly relaxed. Though he hadn't been presumptuous enough to predict the evening would end this way, it had come as no surprise to him to discover that, along with her many other attributes and eccentricities, Stevie was a passionate and sensual woman.

In those fantasies that had haunted his nights since he'd gotten to know Stevie, he'd always imagined that making love with her would be an adventure. Hard as it was to believe, the reality had been even more spectacular. Fact was, just looking at her sleeping now made him harden again, already impatient to see if it would be just as mind-blowing the next time. He'd never met anyone quite like Stevie. Being on the receiving end of her enthusiastic passion was decidedly flattering. A heady ego boost for an innately introverted computer nerd. He couldn't help but smile.

A guy could spend a lifetime getting to know and appreciate all the facets of Stevie. He lifted his left hand, and the band on his finger gleamed softly in the dim light. He wasn't at all sorry he'd signed up for this mission. He just hoped he could keep up with her and make sure she never regretted accepting his proposal.

He wasn't her usual artistic type. He was no poet. Couldn't play a musical instrument. Sang like a bullfrog. Couldn't draw a stick figure. He had no expectations of sweeping Stevie off her feet. But he liked the image he'd formed of their future together, the one she'd described for him earlier—coming home from his business trips to a house filled with warmth and light, to the welcome of a woman who rarely stopped chattering and whose laughter was infectious. To a child's hugs and what-did-you-bring-mes?

He would do his best to make Stevie happy with what he had to offer in return for the family he'd thought he'd never have. He'd be there for her, take care of her even when she didn't know she needed it. That was what he did.

As for what he would receive in return . . . He brushed a light kiss against her warm, damp cheek, certain he'd gotten the best of this bargain. In addition to the cozy family home he'd just envisioned, he had more nights in bed with Stevie to look forward to. Considering how spectacular their first time had been, he was eagerly anticipating the next. He had a feeling he had just begun to explore all the fascinating facets of this woman who was now his wife.

After a surprisingly sound night's sleep, Stevie woke slowly, stretching and yawning before she opened her eyes to find Cole watching her with a smile. A little gasp escaped her before her sleep-clouded mind cleared enough to remind her of why he was there.

He reached out to touch her arm. "That's twice in the past week I've startled you out of sleep. I feel as though I should apologize again."

Rubbing her eyes, she laughed ruefully. "It's not your fault. I just tend to wake up disoriented."

"I'll keep that in mind in the future," he murmured.

She blinked a few times at the reminder of a future that included him now. "Oh, my gosh!"

His left eyebrow rose. "What?"

Struggling to sit up, she pushed at her tangled hair with a rueful little laugh. "Like I said, I wake up disoriented. I just remembered we got married yesterday."

Rising onto his elbow, he looked at her with both brows lifted now. A grin tugged tentatively at the corners of his lips, though he looked as if he wasn't sure whether he should laugh. "I'm not surprised you're befuddled. It all happened pretty fast."

She smiled to show him she recognized the humor in her admission. "You could say that again. Thursday morning I woke up thinking I'd be a single mom and by Friday afternoon I was a married woman. I mean, I've acted on impulse more than a few times in my life, but—oh, my gosh."

He did chuckle then. "You think it's hard for *you* to believe? Even after I'd spent several days considering the idea, I didn't really expect to be married within twenty-four hours of proposing. It just sort of happened. I'm not calling it an impulse, though. More like a plan of action expedited for maximum benefit."

Laughing, she cupped his face in her hands and murmured against his lips, "I just love it when you talk all analyst-y."

"I'm not sure that's a—"

She kissed him before he could finish the sentence.

Showing that he was still open to spontaneity—or, as he would consider it, efficiently taking advantage of an impromptu opportunity—he flipped her onto her back and rolled on top of her. Her delighted laughter quickly changed to murmurs of pleasure as he proved once again that her math genius husband was as clever with his mouth and hands as he was with that brilliant mind.

They enjoyed a leisurely breakfast at a farmhouse-style diner, during which Stevie chattered about trips to Branson as a child with her mother and brother. Cole mentioned that he'd visited only a few times himself, the first trip as a very young boy with his parents during one of their attempts to act the part of happy family— an attempt she surmised hadn't been particularly successful, though he didn't elaborate.

Taking advantage of a chilly, but otherwise beautiful day, they wandered through attractions and shops after breakfast. They were strolling at a leisurely pace through an outlet shopping center when Cole drew her into a store that specialized in baby supplies. An odd feeling gripped her as she drifted down the aisles beside him, rather intimidated by all the merchandise surrounding them. There seemed to be so much of it, so many options, colors, sizes. Was all this stuff necessary for one little baby? She didn't even know what some of these things were. Insecurity rose up in her. Shouldn't she know?

"Stevie? Are you okay? You look a little pale."

She tried to force a reassuring smile for Cole, who gazed down at her in concern. "Just a little overwhelmed. I don't even know how to use most of this stuff."

He placed a hand on the small of her back. "You'll learn what you need to know."

She wished she felt as confident as he sounded. She gave a determined nod. "I'll learn."

"Have you decided which bedroom will be the nursery?"

"The one I've been using as a guest room, I suppose—the one that was mine growing up. It's close to the master, and I've been using the third bedroom as a home office. Um, my house is a little bigger than yours, so it makes sense for us to set up there, right?"

He nodded. "I can keep my office in my house for now, but we'll probably want to discuss combining our households into a larger place eventually. One that will accommodate two offices and a guest room."

She wasn't ready to discuss selling or buying houses just then. It was a given that they would live together in one house, of course. After all, they were married.

She changed the subject quickly when she spotted a white wicker bassinet with a sage-and-off-white chevron-stripe liner. "Oh, look, Cole. Isn't it pretty?"

"That's the same color green you've used in your house, isn't it?"

"Sage. It's my favorite." She was already stroking the little bed, picturing it in a sage-and-cream nursery suitable to either gender. She could find some vintage nursery prints to frame for the walls, and invest in a comfortable nursing chair in a soft nubby fabric with one of her late maternal grandmother's hand-knit throws draped over the back. The turtle night-light would sit on an antique nightstand beside the crib. Perfect. "And look, it's on sale!"

This little basket was definitely going home with her.

"I've got this." Cole was already signaling for assistance from a clerk. "Is there anything else you want here? What about that little bouncy seat thing over there? The pad is the same shade of green, right? One of my friends swore his daughter was only happy when she was sitting in her bouncy seat after nursing. There's room in the back of the SUV for both the bassinet and that, if you like it. Maybe a few other items, if you see anything else you want."

He was already reaching for his wallet. Stevie shook

her head, moving to stand between him and the bassi-net. "No, I've got it. You've done enough already this weekend."

"Not that much," he assured her. "I've provided a honeymoon of sorts for my bride. Now I'd like to get a few things for the baby."

"No. *I* want to buy this."

He went still, frowning as he studied her firmly de-termined expression. "Why?"

"Because it's my—" Realizing what she'd almost said, she bit her tongue before she could complete the blurted sentence.

Cole's hand fell to his side and he took a step back. His voice turned cool. "All right. Get what you want and I'll help you load it into the car."

She'd hurt his feelings. Guilt flooded through her with the realization. That had been the last thing she'd wanted to do. She needed Cole to understand that though their marriage was based on his selfless offer to help her raise this child, she had no intention of tak-ing advantage of his innate generosity. She'd been in-dependent for more than a decade. She'd married him to be a partner to her, not for financial support. They hadn't had time yet to talk about money or the other day-to-day responsibilities of marriage, but she knew it wasn't going to be easy for her to adjust to his new role in her life. To learn to lean on someone else for a change.

Before she could figure out how to apologize for her thoughtlessness, a salesclerk approached with a bright, friendly smile. "Can I help you?"

Conceding that this was the wrong time and place for a momentous discussion, Stevie purchased the bassi-net and bouncy seat, then helped Cole carry them to his SUV. She wondered if he'd be mad at her, but quickly found he'd masked any feelings behind an easy smile. He even teased her about having to leave his suitcase behind if they bought much more on this trip. Apparently he was determined to put their brief clash behind them, intent on keeping this day a pleasant one. She was glad; it was their honeymoon, after all. Practical discussions could wait until later.

Glancing at his watch, he asked if she wanted to eat dinner before the musical variety show they would be attending that evening.

"Oh, my gosh, yes!" She pressed a hand to her stomach. "I'm starving. I'd never make it through the show without food. For the past couple of weeks, it seems like I'm hungry all the time."

He chuckled and opened her door for her. "As the old saying goes, you're eating for two now. What would you like?"

"Anything that sounds good to you. I'm not picky."

"We'll even find a place with silverware this evening," he assured her, then closed the door.

Watching him round the front of the SUV to the driver's seat, she was relieved he'd put that momentary awkwardness behind them so easily. She supposed she shouldn't be surprised. Cole wasn't one to let emotions rule his actions, something that was difficult for her even when she wasn't flooded with early-pregnancy hormones.

This was all going to work out, she promised herself. It was only to be expected that there would be some compromises in the process. But now that they'd gotten this first minor clash out of the way, she just knew the rest of their honeymoon would be nothing but enjoyable.

Cole stood beside the bed a few hours later, feeling helpless as Stevie curled into a ball and moaned. He'd dimmed the lights for her comfort, but even in the shadows her skin still seemed to have a slightly green tint to it. "Is your stomach still upset?"

The only response to his tentative question was another heartfelt groan.

He moved to the sink where he dampened a washcloth with cold water, then carried it back to her. "Let me put this on your throat. My grandma used to do that for me when I was nauseated and it always seemed to help."

She shifted on the thick pillows and allowed him to press the cloth gently to her throat. "I'm sorry," she murmured, her eyes squeezed shut. "I didn't mean for the evening to end this way."

"Don't apologize. I'm just sorry you're ill. Are you sure we shouldn't have you checked by a doctor?"

She shook her head and managed a weak smile as she peered up at him through barely cracked eyelids. "No. It's just nausea. I guess I bragged too soon about not being sick a day so far. At least we made it to the end of the show."

But only just, he thought with a wry shake of his head. He'd noticed Stevie had seemed subdued at intermission. At first he'd wondered if it was because he'd somehow annoyed her at the baby supplies store earlier, though they'd gotten along fine during dinner. But she'd confided that she was feeling a little queasy, so he'd bought her a soda to sip while the energetic young singers and dancers had taken the stage for the second half. He'd only halfway paid attention to the stage, surreptitiously watching Stevie instead as she'd wilted visibly in her seat. He'd all but carried her to the car afterward, and she'd barely made it into the room before bolting into the bathroom and slamming the door behind her. When she'd reemerged, it was only to collapse on the bed, still fully clothed.

He slipped off her shoes and set them on the floor. "Would you like to put on your nightgown?"

Her eyes were closed again, but he thought there might be a bit more color in her face now. "I'll change in a minute," she murmured.

He moved to the dresser. She'd brought a couple of nightgowns—one made of black satin, the other a warmer purple knit splashed with cheery red flowers. As diverse as the two garments were, each somehow seemed perfectly suited to Stevie. Though his hand lingered for a moment on the black one, he pulled out the more comfortable-looking gown and carried it to the bed. "Here, let me help you," he said.

A few minutes later, she was snugly tucked into the bed, the washcloth redampened and draped again on her throat. "Can I get you anything else? Some more soda?"

She shifted on the piled pillows, moistening her lips. "Maybe a little."

Sitting beside her on the bed, he handed her the glass of citrusy soda he'd purchased from a vending machine down the hall. She took a couple of sips, then gave it back to him. "Thanks. I feel better now. Just tired."

"I'll sleep on the sofa bed."

She shook her head and patted the bed next to her. "I'm hardly contagious. You'll be much more comfortable here in this king-sized bed than on that fold-out."

He wasn't so sure about that, considering she'd be snoozing beside him, temptingly close but needing her rest. Still, as she'd said, it was a big bed. It had been a long time since he'd shared a bed with anyone, and he had to admit he liked the feel of a warm, soft body next to him even if only in sleep.

She was mostly out by the time he climbed in beside her, taking care not to jostle the mattress or otherwise disturb her. He'd hardly settled onto the pillows before she turned and snuggled into him, her hair tickling his chin, her small hand resting on his chest. He wore pajama bottoms and a T-shirt, but he could feel her warmth through the fabric. Too warm? He rested a hand lightly against her face, reassuring himself that she wasn't running a fever.

"I'm fine," she murmured drowsily, and he wasn't sure she was actually awake. "I just never want to smell popcorn again."

He stroked a wayward curl off her cheek. There was no need to reply. She wouldn't have heard him, anyway, as she'd already drifted off again.

On impulse, he pressed a light kiss on the top of her head, then tried to relax. It wasn't easy. Even discounting the distraction of having her in his arms, he was having trouble turning off his thoughts. He kept replaying the day, from the exhilarating wake-up sex to that terse exchange in the baby store. He still wasn't sure exactly why she'd taken such exception to his offer to buy the bassinet and seat. He wasn't very good at reading emotional cues, being the type who preferred issues plainly spelled out. But he thought maybe he'd unwittingly stepped on her pride.

He hadn't tried to imply that she wasn't capable of providing for her child. He hadn't been trying to take charge or insist on having his own way. He'd simply wanted to show her that he shared her excitement about the baby.

Her baby, he reminded himself with a wince. It had been clear enough what she'd started to say before she'd swallowed the words. For all her talk about sharing the child with him, about commitment mattering more to her than biology, for all the nervous enthusiasm she'd shown so far toward their marriage even to the point of eagerly consummating their wedding night, there was still a part of herself she was holding back from him. A self-protective door that she hadn't yet unlocked, perhaps because of her past disappointments. And she didn't yet trust him enough to open that door for him.

He had to admit it had hurt when she'd snapped at him. When he'd realized what she'd almost said. *Her* baby. Not theirs. The words had hit him like a blow, though he'd tried to hide his reaction to keep the peace.

Because he wasn't one to dwell on injured feelings, he relied instead on his usual method for dealing with uncomfortable emotions. Objective analysis. He needed to be patient. This was all so new for both of them. In the long run, he still believed he and Stevie would make a success of this marriage. That they and the child they'd raise together would have a good life. A contented life.

He'd have to proceed cautiously, prove to her that he was here for the long term. That he would not walk away from her when life got difficult. With time, he would convince her that she could trust him completely. And that she and her child—their child—could rely on him. Always.

Chapter Five

The pale winter sunlight just seeped around the edges of the window curtains when Stevie woke Sunday morning. She turned her head to find Cole still sleeping beside her. Had he lain awake awhile after she'd fallen asleep? She certainly hadn't intended to cut their second night short that way. She was just relieved she'd made it through to the end of the show.

She slid carefully from the bed and padded into the bathroom, silently closing the door behind her. Fortunately there was no nausea this morning, so she felt much more herself when she emerged a few minutes later. She tiptoed back into the room, but it turned out not to be necessary. Cole was awake, propped against the pillows with his hands behind his head, watching her as she stepped into the room.

Smoothing her palms down the front of her red-flowered purple gown, she smiled at him. "Hey."

"Hey. Feeling better?" His voice was a deep, sleep-roughened rumble in the quiet room. Her throat closed in response.

He'd been so sweet last night when she'd been ill, taking care of her without hesitation. He had a lot of experience as a caregiver, of course—but she wasn't accustomed to being the one on the receiving end. She felt a sudden need to assure him that she really was fully recovered.

"I feel great this morning," she said as she approached the bed.

"The color's back in your cheeks and your eyes are bright again." He nodded in satisfaction as he studied her face. "You looked wrung out last night."

"Here's a hint, Cole." She sat on the bed beside him and leaned over him, her hands on his chest. "Don't mention that your new bride looked sickly on her honeymoon."

He chuckled and ran his hands up her arms. "Sorry. If it makes any difference, I still had trouble keeping my hands to myself when I helped you into this nightgown."

"Yes, that's much better," she assured him, giving in to an impulse to run a hand through his thick tousled hair. "Did I mention I'm perfectly fine now?"

With a grin, he tugged her into his arms. "I'm happy to hear that. For several reasons."

Her laughter was smothered by his hungry kiss.

Holding a bag in one hand, Stevie looked around the hotel room as they prepared to depart later that morning, her gaze lingering for a moment on the big bed. She found herself suddenly reluctant to leave this private retreat. Reality waited outside this door—the tasks of informing all their friends and families of their marriage and dealing with the reaction, figuring out how to combine their households, learning to live together, coordinating schedules in preparation for the baby's arrival…

She took a deep breath and stopped listing the tasks before she became completely overwhelmed. *One step at a time, Stevie.*

Cole stepped up behind her and rested a hand on her shoulder. "Ready to go?"

"No."

His fingers tightened reassuringly for a moment. "It will be fine."

She smiled faintly up at him. "I know. But it's been nice here."

He leaned his head down to brush a kiss over her lips. "I'd like to stay longer, too," he admitted when he stepped back. "Unfortunately…"

"The honeymoon is over," she finished, turning toward the door.

Cole gave a little grimace. "Maybe I wouldn't have phrased it quite that way," he murmured as he opened the door to the hallway.

Giving him a look of wry apology, she preceded him out of the room.

"Is there anything else you want to do before we head out of town?" he asked after a leisurely breakfast.

"Yes."

"More shopping? Another show?"

She smiled. "Let's just say it will involve a wager."

She noted that he looked both intrigued and a little wary in response, which made her laugh.

An hour later, she faced him with her shoulders squared, chin held confidently high. "Well? Still feeling good about that bet?"

"Pretty sure that was an unfair challenge." Cole tilted

his head as he eyed her in suspicion. "How many times have you played this course?"

Smiling nostalgically, she glanced around the indoor miniature golf course. The large space was dimly illuminated. Two eighteen-hole courses were lit by low walkway lights with multicolored plastic shades. Tiny fairy lights were strung in greenery arranged to replicate a nighttime garden setting. Tinkly new age music played from hidden speakers, and water splashed in artificial streams and falls, creating a mystical ambiance that explained why the few other players on this Sunday morning spoke in quiet tones, their laughter politely muted.

Holding putters, Stevie and Cole faced each other across the tee of the eighteenth hole. Only one stroke separated their scores, the advantage hers.

"I can't remember how many times, exactly," she said in answer to his question. "But every time Mom brought us to Branson for vacations, Tom and I begged her to let us play in here and in the arcade down the hall. We always bet on the outcome—doing dishes for a week, putting away the laundry, various household chores. Mom wouldn't let us bet money."

"You still haven't told me what we're wagering," he reminded her, his tone indulgent. "And by the way, I don't actually mind doing household chores."

"So, what are you offering if I win?"

He gave it a moment's thought, taking advantage of having no one behind them and waiting to play to stretch out the teasing conversation. "If you win, I'll wash and detail your car when we get home."

Having known her for a year, he was aware of how much she hated washing her car, and it was especially dirty after last week's snow and mud. "Ooh. Interesting."

He chuckled, tossing and catching his bright yellow golf ball in his right hand. "And what will you do for me if I win?"

She bit her lower lip for a moment in thought, then spread her hands, offering a vague pledge she was pretty sure she wouldn't have to make good. "If you win, I'll owe you a favor to be redeemed at your discretion. You name it."

His eyebrows rose. "Sounds intriguing. But you look awfully confident you won't have to pay up. You're pretty good at this next hole, huh?"

"Scared?"

He dark eyes gleamed with amusement. "Maybe."

He really was cute. More relaxed than she'd been in weeks, she grinned back at him. "Well?"

He swept a hand toward the course. "Take your shot."

Already picturing her car all shiny and clean, inside and out, she bent to place her hot pink golf ball on the rubber mat. As she did so, she glanced over her shoulder at Cole. Was he admiring the curve of her bottom? He looked away quickly and she thought his face might have flushed just a little, though it was hard to tell in the shadowy venue. Biting her lip against a smile, she stood and lined up her shot.

A short while later, she walked out of the golf course into a big indoor breezeway, still shaking her head in disbelief. Smiling from ear to ear, Cole wrapped an arm around her shoulders. "So now you owe me a big favor."

"I still can't believe you got a hole in one. And that I whiffed that last putt. Are you sure you weren't just taking it easy on me on the first seventeen holes?"

"I just got lucky with the hole in one, and you only missed your second putt by a half inch."

"So what's my penalty? Have you decided what you want for the bet you won?"

"Not yet. I'll let you know when I think of it."

She looked up at him through her lashes, enjoying his lazily teasing mood despite her pretend pouting. "Now I'm the one who's scared."

He laughed softly and gave her shoulders a little squeeze. "Don't worry, Stevie, I won't have you wash my car."

She made a show of wiping her brow in relief, drawing another laugh from him.

In addition to the mini golf courses and arcade, the building housed a restaurant, a couple of small theaters and several gift shops. Stevie paused to admire a display of scarves, momentarily tempted by their bright colors, sparkly threads and fluttering fringe. Making herself turn away without buying, she looked around for Cole, spotting him standing in front of a display of stuffed animals.

He held a stuffed tiger in his right hand when she joined him. The toy looked quite suitable for an infant, more funny than fierce, incongruously whimsical in Cole's strong hand.

She smiled. "You found a tiger."

He nodded, his expression a little odd. "It caught my eye."

Still he didn't move. She lifted her eyebrows in question. "Are you buying it?"

"Is that okay with you?"

She didn't know whether to sigh or wince in response to his hesitation. "Of course it's okay with me. I think it's adorable."

"Then I'll get it. A souvenir of our honeymoon for the kid."

She chewed her lower lip as she watched him pay for the toy. Had she overreacted about the bassinet yesterday? Or had she merely shown that her independence hadn't changed simply because she now wore Cole's ring on her left hand?

Transaction complete, Cole turned to her. "Ready to head home?"

Forcing a smile, she nodded. "I guess it's time."

They shared a long look before moving in unison toward the exit. Stevie wondered if Cole had been able to read the emotions in her eyes better than she'd been able to decipher his. Probably. She seemed to be an open book to him, while she saw only what he chose to reveal to her.

She figured she had years ahead of her to figure him out. It might just take that long.

They were halfway back to Little Rock when Cole cleared his throat to catch Stevie's attention. She'd been gazing out the side window at the winter-bleak scenery, but barely paying attention to the landmarks. She knew she'd been uncharacteristically quiet, her thoughts focused on the busy and complicated days ahead of them.

"Stevie?"

She glanced around at him when he spoke. "Yes?"

"We'll be passing my dad's place in another twenty minutes or so. Would you mind if we stop and say hello? Might as well get this introduction over with. We won't stay long."

She noted that he didn't look particularly enthusiastic about the prospect. "You want me to meet your father? Now?"

He shrugged. "Now's as good a time as any, since we'll be passing by, anyway."

"Should you call and make sure he's home?"

"He's home."

"Should you at least let him know we're coming?"

"No need. He and I don't stand on formalities."

She almost sighed at how little information he was offering, even though he was the one who'd made this suggestion. "Is there anything more I should know before I meet him?"

Cole shrugged. "I don't expect you to like him very much. Though I guess if anyone could charm Jim McKellar, it would be you."

It didn't reassure her that he sounded less than optimistic.

The house was a modest buff brick bi-level half a mile off the highway outside of Conway. A chain-link fence surrounded the closely cropped, but sparsely landscaped yard. Outside the fence was a large graveled lot filled almost to capacity with vehicles of many makes, models and vintages waiting to be serviced in one of the three metal garages, each with three service bays, lining the lot. Only one of the bay doors was open. A sign over a regular-sized door at one end of the nearest building read McKellar Auto Service and beneath that, in smaller letters, Office.

Stevie saw no activity around the business, which was no surprise at almost five p.m. on a Sunday. She expected Cole to park close to the house. Instead, he pulled into an empty parking space in front of the office.

"That door's up," he explained when he saw her looking at him in question. "That means he's working. He's out here seven days a week unless something unusual comes up. Precisely at five thirty he goes in the house to wash up for dinner, which he eats while he watches the six o'clock newscasts."

"A man of habit," she commented.

"Very much so."

"It looks as though he's quite successful with his business."

"Oh, yeah. He's damned good at what he does. There's not an engine he can't tear down and rebuild given the right equipment, and he's invested wisely in that."

"Does he ever take vacations? Time off?"

"Not unless someone forces him. There's nowhere Dad would rather be. What he can't understand is why I don't want to be under the hood of a car with him."

Hearing something in his voice, she tilted her head. "He wanted you to go into the business?"

"Yeah. He'd hoped to turn it over to me someday. I guess he took it personally that I never wanted it."

"That's why you and your dad aren't close? Because you didn't want his auto repair business?"

"There've been other issues, but no need to get into those now. Let's get this out of the way." With that grim statement, he opened his door.

Stevie jumped out of her own side without waiting for him to come around. She shivered as cold air surrounded her, seeping through her layered tops and pants. She reached back into the SUV and grabbed her coat, bundling it around her as she followed Cole toward the open bay door. He wore only his pullover and jeans, but he seemed oblivious to the cold even though his breath hung in puffy clouds in front of him as he called out, "Dad?"

In response to Cole's voice, a man emerged from beneath the raised hood of a battered sedan. Shop lights were trained on the car's engine, silhouetting the man in their bright beams, and Stevie had to blink to bring him into focus. Wearing an oil-smeared blue uniform shirt, faded jeans and worn work boots, he looked like an older, more sun-grizzled and life-worn version of Cole. He still had a full head of hair, though it had gone mostly silver and was cut considerably closer than Cole's. He was squarely built, still muscular in his fifties. His dark eyes were deeply set, and the lines of his weathered face seemed to have settled into a permanent scowl.

Wiping his hands on a shop towel, he greeted his son without obvious signs of surprise or pleasure. "Cole."

"How's it going, Dad?"

"Can't complain. You?"

"I'm good." Cole drew Stevie forward. "There's someone I want you to meet. This is my wife, Stevie. Stevie, meet my father, Jim McKellar."

"It's a pleasure to meet you, Mr. McKellar." She gave him a warm smile and held out her right hand.

She might have expected him to show some surprise, but his expression didn't change when he glanced at her outstretched hand then back up at her face. "I'm covered in oil," he said, still scrubbing at his hands with the towel. "Good to meet you, though. When was the wedding?"

If he was hurt that he'd been neither informed ahead of time nor invited to attend, he kept the feeling well hidden. It wasn't hard to figure out where Cole had learned to mask his emotions.

"We were married Friday," Cole replied. "We're on our way home from a short honeymoon in Branson. I thought you'd like to meet Stevie while we were in the area. Is Peggy here? Stevie should meet her, too."

"Peg's gone to some sort of program at her church. Won't be home for a couple hours yet."

"Next time then."

Jim looked around uncomfortably. "You, uh, want some coffee or something? Got some left in the office."

"Not for me. Stevie?"

She shook her head. "No, thank you."

"Guess we could go in the house and sit down," Jim said, though he glanced tellingly at the car he'd been working on.

"We can't stay, Dad. Stevie and I both have to work tomorrow, so we should head on home."

Something flitted briefly across the older man's face in response to Cole's reply, but Stevie wasn't sure if it was relief or a touch of regret. Maybe a complicated mixture of both. Before she could decide, he spoke again. "Glad you stopped by. Congratulations on the marriage. I'll tell Peg you said hello."

Cole nodded. "Yeah, give her our best."

Blinking, Stevie looked in disbelief from son to father and back again. That was it? No hugs or hearty slaps on the back? No questions about how she and Cole had met or when they'd decided to marry? About future plans or current activities? Just "hey, how's it going, see you later?"

She tossed back her hair and spoke up in a bright tone. "Maybe you and your wife can visit us in Little Rock soon, Mr. McKellar. I'd love to meet her. We could treat you to a nice dinner out, get to know each other better."

Her determined friendliness seemed to startle him a little. "We, uh, don't get down that way very often. Guess you can see I've got a lot of jobs going. These folks want their cars back as soon as we can get 'em finished." He cleared his throat, then seemed to feel something more was expected from him. "But y'all can stop by any time. I'm sure Peggy'd like to meet you."

"We'll try to get back soon," Cole said, his tone as stiltedly cordial—and as emotionally distant—as his father's. "We're both pretty busy with work for the next few months, which is why we had so little time for a honeymoon. Stevie owns her own kitchen design business and she's made quite a name for herself in Little Rock."

Jim nodded, though he didn't look notably impressed. She suspected he was one of those men who couldn't imagine there was much more to kitchen design than deciding where to put the refrigerator. He glanced at Cole before asking gruffly, "You still playing around with computers?"

Stevie saw a muscle tighten in Cole's jaw, but he replied evenly, as if the question was one he'd heard too many times to take offense. "Yeah, pretty much."

"That was all the boy was ever interested in," Jim said as an aside to Stevie. "Holin' up in his room with computer games and such. Couldn't get him interested in sports or hunting or fishing, and he sure wasn't getting his hands dirty under the hood of a car."

Cole placed a hand on Stevie's arm, though she wasn't certain if it was for her benefit or his own. "I doubt Stevie wants to hear a list of your disappointments with me, Dad. It's getting dark, so we'd better get back on the road. I'm sure you want to get back to your work."

Jim's eyes narrowed with what might have been a flash of irritation, but he merely nodded and said, "Yeah, I'm trying to finish this one tonight. Y'all take care now." He turned and picked up a wrench.

Cole turned toward the exit, nudging Stevie to move along with him. She looked back over her shoulder as they walked out, but Jim was hidden behind the car hood again.

They were on the road again for less than ten minutes when Cole sighed gustily. "Okay. Let's hear it. You're obviously bursting to express your opinion."

She'd been all but squirming in her seat, her mind whirling with all the things she wanted to say but wasn't sure how to articulate. In response to his urging, the words gushed from her in a flood of exasperation. "Are you kidding me? That's the way you announce to your father that you've gotten married? That's the way he responds? What on earth is wrong with you two?"

Cole didn't look at all surprised by her outburst. "I gave up trying to answer that question a long time ago. I guess Dad and I are just too different to be close. Not that anyone gets close to my dad. He and Peggy get along well enough, but I'd hardly call their relationship a warm and cozy one. She takes care of the house and stays busy with her church. He works, eats the meals she makes him and watches a little TV before he starts again at daylight the next day. The guys who work for him call him a grouch and a perfectionist, but he pays well enough that most of them have been with him quite a while."

"So he's a difficult man. That doesn't mean you should stop trying to have a relationship with him."

"I do try, Stevie." Cole spoke just a bit more sharply this time. "Why the hell do you think I stopped by to introduce you to him? You saw how he acted. Like we were an interruption he had to tolerate before he could get back to work. He couldn't have cared less."

She twisted a curl around one finger, growing

thoughtful as she replayed the awkward encounter in her mind. "I'm not entirely sure that's true. I think he did care. And I think maybe he was gruff because his feelings were a little hurt."

The SUV swerved just a fraction on the road, a clear indication of Cole's surprise. He gripped the wheel more tightly and focused hard on the road ahead. "You're way off base there. Why would his feelings, if he had any, be hurt? He was the first person we told about our marriage, wasn't he?"

"Well, you didn't mention that to him," she reminded him. "For all he was aware, he was the last to know."

"You didn't hear him ask, did you?"

"No. He probably has too much pride for that. That wall between you has gotten so thick I don't think either of you knows how to break through it. Even how to start."

"I did my part. I reached out a hand and as usual, he basically slapped it away because he considers it too clean to be a real man's hand."

For just that moment, Cole's composure slipped enough for her to catch a fleeting glimpse of the old pain that he kept deeply hidden, but he recovered almost instantly. "Let's not talk about this now. It's not the way I want to end our weekend. I'll just assure you that you don't have to worry I'll be anything like my father when it comes to being a dad. He's taught me everything not to do."

She still believed Cole would be a wonderful father. Which didn't mean he wouldn't still carry the scars from his past. Or that those old wounds might not open up again someday in the future, to the detriment of himself and anyone close to him.

Because she could sense it would do no good to keep

pushing him now while the disappointing visit was still so fresh and raw in his mind, she let it go, changing the subject to their upcoming week's schedule, instead. But she was going to think about this quite a bit more, she vowed silently. And maybe she'd figure out a way to help Cole and his dad build a door in that stubborn, pride-strengthened wall.

There was a moment of awkwardness a while later when Cole turned onto the street where they lived. They'd stopped for a nice dinner when they'd arrived in Little Rock because he'd said they were both too tired to cook after the trip. Now that they'd finally arrived home, he didn't seem sure whether to pull into her driveway or his own garage.

"I'll carry the baby things into your house first," he decided, parking in front of her house.

Faced again with the reality of their new living—and sleeping—arrangements, Stevie tried to hide her own attack of nerves behind practicality. "We should go check on Dusty. Do you think she'd adapt to living in my house with us? I don't think cats like change, do they?"

"Beats me. I've never actually owned a cat before. Or should I say, I've never been owned by a cat before."

She laughed. "She does get her wishes across, doesn't she? Let's bring her over and see if she finds my house suitable."

Dusty seemed a bit wary of the move at first, nervously exploring the house while making sure both Stevie and Cole remained nearby. Stevie set up the litter box in the easily accessible laundry area and the food and water bowls in the kitchen, then showed both to the cat, slipping her a couple of treats in the process. Afterward, Cole sat in an armchair in the living room and patted his knee. Dusty jumped up, curled up on his lap and promptly went to sleep, apparently exhausted by the change but content to be back in her favorite place. Her rumbling purr was audible even halfway across the room to Stevie.

"She's a demanding little diva, isn't she?" Cole asked, fondly rubbing his pet's ears. "I'll help put things away in a bit. Just let me sit here with her for a few minutes to reassure her."

She was suddenly a little jealous of the cat. She wouldn't at all mind sitting in Cole's lap and being petted by him. With a wry smile and shake of her head, Stevie turned toward her bedroom. "Take your time and relax. You did all the driving this weekend. I'll just unpack my bag."

Usually, entering her impeccably decorated bedroom was like escaping to a peaceful retreat. This lovely and understated room soothed her, gave her busy mind a rest from the creative demands of her job, from hectic schedules and complex relationships.

She hadn't shared this bed often. Joe had rented a loft downtown, which had suited him better than this sedate, family-friendly neighborhood. He'd called her place boring, his tastes leaning to modern industrial— soaring ceilings, open pipes, exposed bricks and numerous musical instruments.

Shaking her head to clear her mind of the past, she unpacked her bag and put away her things, then combined a couple of drawers to make space for Cole. It would take a while to get everything arranged, of course, but she wanted him to feel immediately welcome.

She walked back into the living room only to stop

short in the doorway to admire the appealing scene that greeted her. Cole was sound asleep in the chair, one hand still resting on the cat dozing in his lap. His hair was rumpled around his face and he looked younger and more unguarded than usual. She had no doubt he would be on his feet instantly if she said his name, but she tiptoed out of the room, leaving him to rest.

The past two days had been as eventful for Cole as they'd been for her, she mused, trying to put herself in his shoes for a moment. Did he feel the weight of his actions on his shoulders, the responsibilities of the promises he'd made to her and her child? Of course he did. That was just who he was. He was going to have to learn to let someone else take care of him occasionally, she thought firmly. Because that was just who *she* was.

Moving as quietly as possible, she settled at the kitchen table with a cup of herbal tea while she checked email and texts on her phone. The phone vibrated in her hand and she checked the caller ID. Seeing one of her two best friends' names on the screen, she moistened her lips. She didn't want to break her big news on the phone, but she didn't want to lie to her friend, either. She hoped neither option would be necessary as she said, "Hi, Tess. What's up?"

"Just checking in. Scott and I just got back from a weekend in New Orleans."

Stevie was a little surprised. "I didn't know you'd planned a New Orleans weekend."

Tess sighed happily. "He surprised me after we left the office Friday by driving straight to the airport for a Valentine's Day getaway. He'd been planning it secretly for weeks, with the help of his brothers' wives. We spent two nights in a lovely hotel in the French Quarter and we hardly mentioned work all weekend. Even though it was a little chilly and it rained quite a bit it was heavenly to get away for a couple of days."

"Nice." And an illustration of how much workaholic Scott's priorities had changed since he'd become engaged to Tess. A whole weekend away from the busy, successful construction business that meant so much to him was definitely a demonstration of his commitment to his bride-to-be. "I'm glad you had fun."

"Now I'm looking forward to our honeymoon," Tess admitted with a laugh. "I can't wait to get on that warm beach in the Cayman Islands after this cold, dreary winter."

Tess and Scott were to be married in mid-June on the spreading back lawn of his parents' West Little Rock home. Their guest list would be as small as they could politely manage, their theme restrained and elegant. A sweet, simple wedding, as Tess frequently described, was her preference. But "simple" was a matter of perspective, Stevie thought wryly, remembering her own little ceremony with Pastor Dave and Luanne.

"Tess…"

Oh, goodness, how to even start?

"Yes?" her friend prodded after a moment.

On a sudden inspiration, Stevie blurted, "Can you come to my place tomorrow evening? Around seven? I know it's short notice, but it won't take long if you have other things you need to do. I'm going to ask Jenny, too."

"A girls' night?" Tess asked after a momentary hesitation that indicated she'd heard something odd in Stevie's voice.

"Not exactly. I'll explain tomorrow, okay? It'll be easier in person. Can you come?"

"I'll make time. Stevie…is something wrong?"

"Everything's good," Stevie assured her. "We'll talk tomorrow."

Her call with Tess completed, she shot a quick text invitation to Jenny, who accepted immediately.

"Everything okay?" Cole asked from the doorway.

She looked up from her phone to find him studying her expression in concern. "I've invited Tess and Jenny to drop by tomorrow evening at seven. I'll tell them everything then."

"Sounds like a good plan. I'll do some work over at my place while they're here to give you privacy for your talk."

Grateful for his understanding, she nodded. "I'll text you after I've explained everything to them. I want you to meet them."

She wasn't sure why he'd never met Jenny and Tess. They'd heard her talk about her neighbor and knew Stevie and Cole had become friends, but they'd never all been in the same place at the same time for introductions. In a way, it was almost as if she'd been keeping her friendship with Cole to herself. Those pleasant evenings over tea with him and his cat—they'd been special to her, she admitted now. She could never have dreamed then where they'd lead, but she'd privately treasured them.

And now it was time to bring those separate components of her life together.

"What about you?" she asked Cole. "Do you have friends you'll want to bring together for the big announcement?"

He shrugged. "I'll spread the word among my friends in the next week or so. I have a few local buddies, but no one as close as Jenny and Tess are to you. I need to call my mother, but I'll wait until the morning since it's an hour later in Florida."

"I should call my mom, too. It's still early enough in Hawaii for me to call her now. I'll send a text to my brother later. He's not much for talking on the phone."

"Sorry I conked out on you in there. Dusty's snoring put me to sleep."

She chuckled. "No problem. You're tired. Where is... oh, here she is."

She reached down to stroke the cat winding around her ankles. Dusty was beginning to look more comfortable in her new quarters now that she'd been reassured her beloved Cole had come with her.

"I emptied a couple of drawers for you on the right side of the dresser. We'll have to rearrange the closet to fit your things, but we can do that later. It's a big walk-in and there's plenty of room for your stuff."

"Thanks. I'll unpack while you call your mom."

Drawing a deep breath for fortitude, she called her mom as soon as she was alone in the kitchen again. Her mother had plans for the evening but she made time to take her daughter's call. Stevie barely gave her mom time to say hello before she burst into a nervous speech. Her words all but tripped over each other as she explained that she had eloped with her next-door neighbor and was expecting a child in August and that she and Cole were looking forward to sharing childcare duties and expected to have a long, successful marriage.

Her mother interrupted only a couple of times to ask her to slow down, but she handled the news with typical equanimity. The baby's parentage didn't come up, not that Stevie had expected it to with her nontraditional mom.

"So you chose to marry," her mom said when she finally had a chance to speak. "That's cool, though you know how I feel about the institution. You're keeping your own name, right? Holding on to your business and your financial independence? Do you have a prenup?"

"Don't worry, Mom," Stevie replied with a wry smile. "It's a completely modern marriage."

"There's no such thing," her mother replied brusquely.

"You'll like Cole, Mom. He's a great guy. And he has a very successful career and owns his own house," she added pointedly.

"That sounds promising," her mother conceded grudgingly. "I hope you'll be happy. And make sure you have a good lawyer."

"Yes, Mother," Stevie said with a grin that had to be audible in her voice.

Her mom's musical laughter came through the phone. "Now you're just being sassy."

"Look who raised me," Stevie retorted affectionately. "You're going to be such a fun grandma."

"Oh, God, don't call me that. Your child can call me Bonnie. Or maybe BonBon. That's cute, right?"

"We'll discuss it. Enjoy your evening."

"Oh, I will. Aloha, sweetie."

"Aloha, Mom."

Cole joined her again a few minutes later, pausing in the doorway to make sure the call was concluded before he walked into the room. "How did your call go?"

"Mom wished us well and told me to keep a good lawyer on call. Oh, and she wants to be called BonBon, not grandma."

He smiled, unoffended by the message. "I have to admit, I'm looking forward to meeting your mother."

"She wants to meet you, too. Would you like some tea?"

"Sounds good, but I'll make it. Why don't you stay off your feet for a while. It's been a long day."

At least he'd had the tact not to tell her she looked tired, though she felt a bit bedraggled. "Tea bags are in the pantry, cups in that cabinet," she said, pointing.

He turned her toward the living room. "I'll find what I need. Go rest."

"You talked me into it."

She told herself she was only going to lie down for a few minutes. She curled on the couch with a throw pillow beneath her head, her legs drawn up in front of her. She was just drifting off when a warm little body settled beside her and a deep, steady purr lulled her to sleep.

She wasn't sure what time it was when Cole woke her with a gentle hand on her shoulder. "It's getting late, Stevie. Want to turn in?"

She opened her eyes, noting that he'd dimmed the lights. The cat wasn't beside her now. "What time is it?"

"After ten. I've been working on my laptop, but I think I'll get some sleep. How are you feeling?"

She yawned. "Okay. Just tired."

"Should I carry you to bed?"

Laughing softly, she climbed to her feet. "As manly and sexy as that sounds, I'll walk."

He rested a hand at the small of her back. "You think I'm manly and sexy?"

"Well, of course." She reached up to pat his cheek sleepily. "Not to mention a cutie."

He grunted. "Let's just leave it at manly and sexy, okay?"

She giggled.

A short while later Cole climbed into her bed beside her and reached out to turn off the bedside lamp. He paused for just a moment with his hand on the switch. "Stevie?"

"Mmm?"

"Have I told you how much I like the way you've decorated your house? Especially this bedroom. It's nice."

The light went out, leaving her to lie awake for a few minutes in the dark, thinking about how funny life could be sometimes.

An unexpected life, she thought, glancing in the direction of her jewelry box. She was certainly living up to that fortune cookie's prediction.

Fortunately, Tess and Jenny arrived together the next evening so Stevie didn't have to go through explanations twice. Cold air swirled into the house with the new arrivals, and they gathered around the crackling fireplace to shed their coats and scarves, which Stevie stashed in the front bedroom before returning to her friends. Her stomach was tied in knots as she wondered what they'd say in response to her news.

"How are you feeling?" she asked Jenny, shamelessly stalling for a moment.

With a little groan and a rueful expression, Jenny pressed her hand to her tummy. "Okay now, but the mornings are bad. I have to downplay how sick I feel, though, because poor Gavin gets so distraught."

That didn't surprise Stevie. She knew how overprotective Jenny's husband was. Jenny and Gavin had been sweethearts at the university all three of them had attended, though a bitter, youthful breakup had separated them for a decade. Stevie had been delighted when fate had brought the couple back together. And now they were married and having a baby together. *Way to go, fate.*

Tess smiled sympathetically, though her expression made Stevie wonder if Tess, too, was imagining a day when she and Scott would welcome a child. Ironically, Stevie was the only one of the three friends who'd been in no particular hurry to have a baby, until that capricious fate had stepped in to change her status.

Her friends were both so blissfully in love. Yet, having seen the pain both had gone through during rocky patches in their courtships, Stevie was relieved that she and Cole were being more practical with their relationship. Going into marriage and parenthood the way she and Cole had, with clearly defined boundaries and goals and expectations, should certainly minimize any chance of heartbreak for either of them. There would be challenges, of course, some disappointments and annoyances. She was quite sure she'd irritate the hell out of him at times, though she wasn't sure he'd tell her if she did. But they would make it work.

She hoped Jenny and Tess would see the logic of those arguments even if they worried that she had been recklessly impulsive again.

She poured tea all around and waited until the others were seated before clearing her throat in preparation to speak. She was a little surprised that neither of her usually sharp-eyed friends had noticed her new rings, but that only showed how distracted they were with their own lives.

So much had changed in the past year, she thought a bit wistfully. So many changes still lay ahead.

Jenny and Tess were looking at her now as if they sensed something momentous was coming. Before she could speak, a plaintive meow sounded from the doorway and Dusty padded warily into the room. The cat had dashed off to hide when the doorbell rang, nervous about the new arrivals. Dusty wasn't accustomed to company, having lived for a year with her somewhat reclusive owner. But she was too needy to remain hidden away for long when there were potential ear rubs waiting in here.

"Stevie, you got a cat?" Tess asked in surprise, holding out a hand to the little tabby who sniffed it with interest. "She's a pretty little thing, isn't she? Er, he?"

"She." Stevie watched with a faint smile as the cat leaped lightly onto the couch between her friends, regally allowing herself to be stroked and admired.

"What's her name?" Jenny asked.

"Dusty."

Jenny's eyebrows rose. "Your neighbor's cat?" she asked, having heard Stevie mention her cat-sitting sessions. "You're keeping her here when he's away now?"

"He isn't away. Dusty lives here now. And, um, so does Cole."

A startled silence followed her revelation. Jenny and Tess looked at her as if neither was quite sure she'd heard correctly.

Jenny recovered first. "Cole lives here? Since when?"

Stevie held up her left hand to display the glittering rings. "Since we eloped Friday afternoon. We got married."

Chapter Six

The quiet in the room was deafening. Stevie could almost hear her own rapid heartbeat as she waited for her friends' reactions. Of all their possible responses, silence was the last thing she expected.

It seemed minutes before Tess roused first from the temporary paralysis. "You're *married*?"

"Yes. For three whole days now." With a look of apology, she sought out the gaze of her oldest friend. "I'm sorry I didn't tell you before. It's just…well, it all happened very fast."

Setting aside her teacup, Jenny rose slowly to her feet. "I can't believe this, Stevie. It's…it's just…I can't believe you're married."

"When did all this come about?" Tess nudged the cat gently out of the way and stood. "You never even hinted that you and Cole were seeing each other."

Stevie twisted her hands in front of her. "It's sort of a

long story. I was going to tell you part of it when we got together last week, but it was the night you announced your pregnancy, Jen. I didn't want to steal your thunder or worry either of you. Cole and I agreed it might be easier for us to elope and tell you everything afterward. Please don't be hurt that I didn't tell you first. As I said, this all came about very quickly, and there was hardly time to make any calls. I didn't even tell my mom until after the wedding."

She watched as her friends exchanged glances that held all the doubts and concerns she'd braced for. "You don't have to look so worried. I knew what I was doing, and I gave it careful consideration."

Okay, maybe she'd given it all of five minutes consideration before she'd accepted Cole's proposal, she thought with a slight wince of memory. Perhaps it would be best not to mention that just now.

"Forgive us for being skeptical," Jenny said slowly, "but, Stevie…have you lost your mind?"

Stevie didn't take offense. She might have said exactly the same thing if the tables had been turned. "No. I have my reasons, Jen, and I think when you hear them you'll agree they're good ones."

"The only valid reason to marry is for love," Jenny retorted flatly. "Aren't you the one who made that declaration repeatedly when I was considering Thad's proposal? You were never enthusiastic about my relationship with him because you said it was too calculated and dispassionate. You were all for me getting back with Gavin despite our differences, because you knew I had always loved him."

"And didn't you nag me to make sure Scott and I were getting married for the right reasons?" Tess chimed in. "You said marriage should be more than a practical business arrangement. You were so insistent that I actually broke off our engagement until Scott was able to convince me he was in love with me. So I hope you have a very good reason for eloping with your neighbor."

"I did marry Cole for love," Stevie assured them, her hand on her stomach. She loved this baby enough to give him or her as many advantages as she could provide, including a man who would dedicate himself to being a wonderful father. She thought her friends would agree there was nothing cold-blooded or calculated about this marriage, despite its functional foundation.

Jenny knew her too well and for too long to simply accept those words at face value. She took a step closer and frowned intently into Stevie's eyes. "You broke up with Joe only three months ago. I knew you weren't particularly heartbroken by that split—and frankly, I thought it was well past time—but you never said a word about having feelings for anyone else. This wasn't a rebound thing, was it? Or were you involved with Cole even then?"

Again, Stevie wasn't insulted by Jenny's personal questions. As both her friends had just reminded her, she'd butted her nose into their affairs a few times, always with the best intentions. Just as they held now toward her. "No. At the time, Cole and I were simply good friends."

"When did that change?"

She drew a deep breath, then confessed, "When I told him I was pregnant and that I was nervous about trying to raise the child alone."

Tess sank abruptly back down onto the couch, as if

this newest surprise had taken the stiffening right out of her knees. "You're pregnant?"

"Yes." She aimed another look of apology toward Jenny. "Now do you understand why it was so hard to tell you on the same night you told us about your baby? You were so thrilled and excited, and I was so happy for you and Gavin. I knew there would be time to share my own news later."

Jenny gripped Stevie's arm as if she couldn't restrain herself any longer. She looked from her face to her waistline and back again, her expression almost comically conflicted. "You're pregnant? You're sure? How far along are you? Do you feel okay? Is Cole happy about the baby?"

A laugh escaping her, Stevie covered Jenny's hand with her own and rested her cheek for a moment against her friend's shoulder in a little hug. "Yes, I'm absolutely sure, and I'm fine. I've only been sick once, and that was this past weekend, probably from too much rich food. Cole is very excited about the baby. He'll be a good dad. He's a great guy, Jen. Smart and dependable and kind, with a dry sense of humor and a generous heart. You'll like him, I promise."

"Where is he?"

"He went next door to his house to give us some privacy for this talk. I told him I'd text him when you were ready to meet him."

"Well, call him over." Jenny bounced a couple of times on the balls of her feet, her lips pursed in what was meant to be an intimidating frown. "I want to get a look at this guy. Maybe rake him over the coals a little to make sure he's worthy of you."

As she texted him, Stevie laughed softly, grateful that Jenny was trying to make the best of this admittedly awkward situation. "Good luck with that. You'll find my husband is not easy to rattle."

"Your husband." Holding the cat now, who'd taken a strong liking to her, Tess still looked dazed. "This is a lot to process in one night. So both my bridesmaids will be in maternity dresses for the wedding."

Relieved that most of the confessions were out of the way—with one notable exception—Stevie nodded. "Looks that way."

"Well, at least that loose, comfortable style I requested should work for both of us," Jenny said with a strained little smile. "We'd better get busy finding the perfect dress that will suit whichever shape Stevie and I happen to be in June."

The opposite of a demanding diva bride, Tess waved a hand. "Pick whatever dress you and Stevie like. As long as it works with the colors I've chosen, I trust your judgment on style."

Jenny nodded. "I'll check with my suppliers and see what I can find in the time we have."

"Yes, well, you and Gavin had a very short engagement, and you thought *my* wedding was short notice," Tess commented with a little laugh. "I'd say Stevie wins this one. She skipped all the wedding prep entirely."

"Cole took care of everything," Stevie admitted. "We had a lovely little Valentine's Day wedding at a cute chapel in the Ozarks. I have a disc of photos that was part of the wedding package. I want to have them printed in one of those glossy photo books when I have time to deal with them."

"I can't wait to see them," Tess said.

Tess was obviously trying hard to show support for Stevie's decision, to look happy about the developments despite whatever concerns she wasn't voicing. Stevie appreciated that, though she wasn't sure she deserved it after keeping her friends in the dark all this time.

Jenny examined Stevie's middle again. "When is your due date? Maybe it's the same as mine. Wouldn't that be something?"

"Um, no." Stevie moistened her lips. "I'm a little farther along than you. I'm due in early August. My tentative due date is August 10."

Jenny looked confused. "August? But that makes you—"

"Three months pregnant."

"Three months," Tess murmured, staring at Stevie's waistline in disbelief. "But you aren't showing."

"I'm getting a little thicker around the middle. I'm wearing loose clothes so it's hard to tell. But I haven't gained much weight yet, though my doctor assured me the baby is developing as it should be."

Comprehension dawned slowly but inevitably on her friends' faces. "But three months ago…"

Stevie held Jenny's gaze without looking away. "That was just before Joe moved to Austin."

"So Joe is…?"

"Out of the picture. Permanently."

Jenny digested that for a moment, then asked quietly, "Does he know?"

"Yes. But it doesn't make a difference. He made his choice. I made mine. I don't think either of us will have any regrets."

"Cole doesn't mind…?"

"Like I said, Cole's looking forward to being a dad to this baby. I married my very good friend, Jen, and we're going to raise a child together. We'll make it work."

"I have no doubt of that," Jenny murmured, her eyes suddenly liquid. "But will you be happy, Stevie? Truly happy? I always thought you'd be crazy in love when you married."

Stevie managed a smile. "You know me. I'm always happy. I'm confident I could have handled all this on my own, just like my mother did, but I'm very fortunate that I'll have a helpmate. That my child, like yours, will have a dad to love and encourage him. Or her."

"It doesn't surprise me that you'd sacrifice everything for your child. That's just so you."

"I don't think of it that way at all," Stevie assured her, equally softly. "Cole is fully committed to this partnership, and I'm so grateful to him. I just hope he doesn't feel that he's the one making the sacrifice."

"I don't."

Stevie almost gasped in response to the deep voice from the doorway leading into the kitchen. She looked around to see Cole standing there, his eyes locked with hers, his expression somber.

"I didn't hear you come in," she said.

"I came in through the back door."

She moved to draw him into the room, standing beside him as they faced her friends. "Jenny, Tess, I'd like you to meet my husband, Cole McKellar."

"Oh, my God." Cole draped himself over a living room chair, his limbs hanging bonelessly, his hair rumpled from being scraped through with both hands. "I've had job interviews complete with FBI background checks that were less grueling."

Reclined on the couch, Stevie laughed. "It wasn't that bad."

"It was that bad. I had the feeling that if I gave one wrong answer, your friend Jenny would throw me out on my ear."

"Just give her a little time to adjust. You have to admit I sort of sprang all this on them."

He opened one eye to look at her. "You think she will? Adjust, I mean?"

"Of course. She already likes you. I could tell, and I know Jen better than anyone. She's just a little worried."

He grew serious. "Your friends seem nice. I figured they would be, from everything you've told me about them."

"You'll like their guys, too. You and Scott have quite a bit in common, actually. He's into tech stuff, too. Always buying new computer equipment for his commercial construction business. Gavin's more into sports and cop stuff, but he's a great guy."

"Cop stuff, huh?"

She shrugged.

"I'll try to find things to talk about with him. Something tells me we'll be spending time with them since you girls are so tight."

"I'd like to meet your friends, too. We haven't talked about them much. Who's your best friend?"

"Probably Joel Bradley. He's an engineer, living and working in Dubai at the moment. He's the one I told you about, my friend from school who was adopted?"

"Of course I remember." He'd said his friend was closer to his adopted family than Cole was to his biological one. Having seen Cole with his Dad, Stevie didn't find that hard to believe now. "Do you hear from Joel much?"

"We stay in touch. Through computers, of course," he added with a wry smile. "It's been a while since we've touched base, but we'll talk again soon."

"And what about your friends here?"

"Sometimes I meet up with a couple of guys from

my gym for beers and conversation. And I'm still tight with some friends from the dojo where I trained for a while. We try to get together once a month for some friendly sparring or *gomoku* tournaments."

"Go—?"

"Gomoku. It's a traditional Japanese board game played with black and white stones. My friends and I are kind of nerdy," he confessed with a chuckle that made no apologies.

Fascinated by this new glimpse into his private life, she prodded, "You said you met at a dojo? You trained in martial arts?"

"Yes."

In the year she'd known him, it was the first she'd heard about this. Swinging her feet to the floor, she studied his face. "What kind?"

"Karate."

"How high did you advance? The belt color thing, I mean?"

"I have a black belt. Second degree."

She felt her jaw drop a little. So that explained why he was in such good shape! "I thought you weren't into sports."

He spread his hands. "Not football or basketball or other organized team sports, particularly, though I've been known to attend a game occasionally with friends. I look at karate more as a way to stay in shape than as a sport. After all, I sit at a computer all day."

She wondered if his father knew about Cole's accomplishment. Jim had been so dismissive of Cole's job and interests, implying that they weren't "manly" enough—but surely a second degree black belt in karate was macho enough to satisfy even Jim McKellar's old-fashioned gender expectations. More than likely

Cole hadn't mentioned it. He didn't seem to need to prove anything to his hard-to-please dad, nor need to defend his masculinity. He'd never even mentioned his accomplishments to her.

"Can you break a stack of boards with your fist?"

He smiled. "I've been known to split a few."

She cocked her head and pictured him barefoot in the traditional white wrap jacket and loose pants, a black belt wrapped around his taut waist, his hair and face damp with sweat as he squared off against an opponent. A jolt of sexual attraction shot through her in response to the image. Interesting. And unexpected, considering what she'd once considered her "type." She'd certainly never before envisioned her quiet, cat-owning, math-whiz neighbor as a tough, sweaty warrior.

He frowned. "Why are you staring at me as if you've never seen me before?"

"Sorry, was I? You're just turning out to be full of surprises, Cole Douglas McKellar."

His lips quirked into a half smile. "Just trying to stay healthy."

"Do you still train?"

"Other than the casual sparring, no. I wasn't interested in competing in tournaments and that would be the next step."

"I'll have to work off the baby weight after Peanut arrives. Maybe I should take up karate."

His grin made her wonder just what amused him so much. Couldn't short, busty women wear white pajamas and kick things?

But he changed the subject before she could challenge him. "By the way, I finally connected with my mom this afternoon. Told her we were married and expecting a kid."

The latter fact was one he'd neglected to mention to his father, she remembered. "How did your mom react?"

"She's pleased with the prospect of being a grandmother. She said she and Ned would head this way in a few months to visit, once the weather gets warmer."

"She didn't mind that she wasn't invited to the wedding?"

"No. Not when I told her no one else was there, either."

"Good." She'd have hated to get off on the wrong foot with her mother-in-law.

He rubbed his chin. "Your friend Tess is planning a big wedding, isn't she?"

"They're trying to keep it contained, but Scott has a big family and a ton of business associates. Tess's family is smaller, but her friends and relatives want to be there, too."

After a moment, he asked, "Are you sorry you didn't have a more traditional wedding so your friends could stand up with you?"

"No," she said and hoped he believed her. "I much prefer our sweet little ceremony. I wouldn't have minded having Tess and Jenny there, but if we'd invited them, others might have been hurt, so it's best we kept it just the two of us."

"I just don't want you to feel that I prevented you from having the wedding you wanted."

"You didn't talk me into anything I didn't want to do," she said, meeting his eyes. "I'd think you should know by now that I make my own choices."

He conceded with a nod, though he didn't look particularly gratified.

An uncomfortable stillness fell over the room. Stevie felt as if there were more things he wanted to say.

More things she perhaps needed to say. She just couldn't think of them at the moment.

She pushed herself to her feet. "I have a meeting with a client tomorrow afternoon. I think I'll go over my notes for a while. Unless you need something?"

"You don't have to entertain me, Stevie. I live here now, remember? I have some reading to do. Might watch some TV for a while. We're good."

We're good.

For some reason those two words made her feel somewhat better as she moved into her office.

Cole couldn't focus on either work or television for the next hour, though both the TV and computer screens flickered in front of him. His thoughts were focused on Stevie and on the snippet of conversation he'd heard earlier.

He hadn't liked Jenny's suggestion that Stevie had sacrificed herself for her child's sake by marrying him. He thought they were doing very well so far. He enjoyed having meals with her, planning a future with her, waking up beside her. He especially liked making love with her. He was already starting to picture himself teaching their kid about science, math and computers, about classic sci-fi and the basics of martial arts training. All the "nerdy" things he longed to share. Stevie would impart her love of music, her creativity, her humor and joyous spontaneity, her people skills and business acumen. Between the two of them, the kid would have a well-rounded foundation.

He was even starting to feel less guilty—a little—that he was moving on in his life, putting past regrets behind him and looking forward to a new, rewarding future.

* * *

Pepper Rose was rapidly becoming one of Stevie's all-time favorite design clients. Despite the name Pepper herself cheerfully termed a "classic stripper name," she was a brilliant and highly respected neuropsychiatrist affiliated with the medical school in Little Rock. Sixty years old, defiantly flame-haired, a few pounds overweight but energetic and light on her feet, Pepper had insisted on the use of first names as their collaboration continued.

"Just don't call me Dr. Pepper," she'd added with a weary smile. "You have no idea how tired I get of that particular joke."

"I can imagine," Stevie had responded with a laugh.

Married to a cardiologist, Pepper had recently cut back on her formerly grueling work schedule and was now involved in remodeling the home she and her husband had purchased a few months earlier. Built on a tall bluff with a breathtaking view of the Arkansas River below and the distant rolling hills beyond, the house was luxurious but a bit sterile in decor, especially in the white-on-white-on-stainless contemporary kitchen.

"Color," Pepper had said when Stevie asked the first thing she wanted changed. "Please give me some color. I don't care about trends or fashion, I just don't want to feel like I'm still in a hospital setting when I walk into my kitchen in the morning."

Stevie had embraced the challenge of designing a kitchen that was functional, fashionable and still incorporated Pepper's love of color—most particularly, the color purple.

"Oh, Stevie, you've found it!" Pepper exclaimed at this meeting in her home late Tuesday afternoon. "This is the ideal granite for my countertops. I can't believe it."

Almost smugly, Stevie patted the granite sample she'd brought with her. Mottled shades of gray with a subtle purple veining, the granite hadn't been easy to locate, but she'd known when she'd found it that it was exactly what Pepper wanted. Though Pepper had tentatively approved a blueprint for the remodel, the multitude of other choices had been put on hold until Stevie located the perfect granite.

"We can keep the backsplash neutral or pull out more of the purple. I've also located a set of pendant lights for over the island that I think you'll love, but we'll have to order them quickly if you want them. They're a little pricey, but still just within the lighting budget." She turned her tablet toward her client to better display the photo of the unique pendants formed of hand-blown purple glass.

"They're gorgeous. Order them." Typically, cost meant little to Pepper, though she and her husband had determined a top dollar for the remodel project. "Stevie...is there something you haven't told me?"

Looking up from the tablet screen, Stevie searched her mind for any other kitchen item she'd forgotten. "What do you mean?"

Pepper reached out to touch Stevie's left hand. "I don't remember seeing these before."

Her gaze drawn to the rings, Stevie nodded in comprehension. She felt her cheeks warm a little. "Oh. Yes, I was married last Friday."

"And you're working today?" Pepper clicked her tongue in disapproval.

"We're delaying our honeymoon for now," she answered lightly. "It's a busy time for both of us in our careers."

"Congratulations on your marriage. I hope you'll be very happy. And I hope he knows how lucky he is."

Stevie smiled. "Thank you, Pepper."

"Philip and I will celebrate our thirty-fifth anniversary next month. We were both still in medical school when we married. It's hard to believe the time has passed so quickly."

"Congratulations to you, too. That's quite a milestone."

Thirty-five years. She couldn't even imagine that far ahead in her own marriage.

Pepper gave a little shrug. "I won't pretend we never had a rough time keeping it together. It wasn't always easy balancing two very demanding careers and two inflated egos, along with the challenges of marriage and raising our two daughters. We were fortunate to be able to hire nannies and housekeepers to assist us, but there were plenty of times when I was ready to pull out my artificially red hair," she added cheerfully. "Philip didn't have enough left to pull by the time he was thirty."

Stevie laughed softly. "It's still quite an accomplishment to have a successful career and a successful marriage."

"I'm glad we made it through. Now that our daughters are grown and we've started spending a few less hours at work, there are quite a few things we'd like to do together. Visit our little grandson in Tucson. Travel around Europe. See Australia and New Zealand. We've just never had the time."

"That all sounds wonderful." She wondered if she and Cole would do things like that someday. After this baby was out of the nest, would they be a couple who wanted to share adventures together? Or would they be more like Cole's father and stepmother—he still immersed in his solitary work, she pursuing her own interests for the most part? She didn't like that option. Could either of them really be happy settling for that?

"Stevie? Is everything okay?"

She schooled her expression quickly, reminding herself of her client's profession. It wasn't easy to fool a psychiatrist, especially for someone like her who wore her emotions close to the surface, anyway. "Yes, thank you. It's all still very new, of course, so we have some adjustments to make, but Cole and I are looking forward to setting up our household and starting our family. We've, um, actually gotten an early start on that. I'm expecting a baby in August."

"Well, congratulations again." Pepper looked genuinely delighted. "You'll be a wonderful mother."

"You think so?"

"I know so." Pepper patted her hand again. Then, seeming to sense that Stevie wanted to change the subject, she reached for the tablet. "Now, about these cabinets. Paint or wash?"

Relieved to be brought back into her area of expertise, Stevie pushed her concerns to the back of her mind and focused on her business.

Breathing heavily, Cole tugged off his head gear and ran a hand through his sweat-dampened hair before mopping at his face with a small towel. His friend Russ Krupistsky dropped to the mat at Cole's feet, dragging in breath as he rested with his knees drawn up in front of him. "Good match, Cole," he said, his voice still raspy from exertion.

"Yeah, you, too." Cole reached down to shake Russ's outstretched hand.

He'd met with five others for the monthly meeting

at the dojo where he'd studied karate. It was Thursday evening, and the place was closed for lessons, but the owner encouraged these gatherings of former and current students who wanted to stay in touch. They chipped in to compensate Sensei Tim, deeming the exercise and fellowship worth the nominal cost.

Having refereed the bout and declaring Cole the winner, though by only a very slim margin, Tim gave him a couple of hearty pats on the back. "Good job, Cole. You're staying in good shape for a computer guy."

Cole laughed. "Thanks, Sensei. I do my best."

His broad, dark face creased with a grin, black eyes glinting with humor, Tim reached down a hand to help Russ to his feet, already making a few suggestions for Russ's next bout. When he wasn't formally teaching, Tim was easygoing and jovial. Put him at the head of a class, though, and he barked out orders and corrections with the sharp precision of the army drill sergeant he'd once been.

"Hey, Cole." Her white gi belted snugly around her, Jessica Lopez touched his arm to get his attention. Her brown ponytail hung limply and her cheeks glistened from exertion, but she was smiling. "That was a nice side kick that took Russ down."

"Thanks. I saw you sparring with Gabriel. Looked like you were holding your own."

Jessica, who was somewhere in her late twenties, chuckled wryly. "Considering he's nearly a decade younger and a helluva lot faster than I am, holding my own was the best I could do. But he took it easy on me and I had fun."

"That's what we're here for, isn't it?"

She nodded, ponytail bobbing. "So, Cole... Gabe and Russ and Nick and I thought we'd go have a burger or something when we're done here. We've worked off the calories, right?"

She laughed and he smiled in response, preparing for the inevitable next question.

"Would you like to join us?"

It wasn't the first time in the past few months that he'd suspected Jessica was interested in him, and not just as another member of the gang. He was kind of dense at times when it came to social signals, but even he recognized when a woman was letting him know she wouldn't mind spending time with him.

"Thanks, but I'll have to pass this time. My wife is waiting at home for me."

My wife. The words still felt a little odd on his tongue, even though he'd been married before. It was just taking a little time to grow accustomed to thinking of Stevie in that way.

Jessica's eyes widened dramatically. "Your wife?"

"Dude, you got married?" Russ asked, overhearing. "When did this happen?"

"Last week." He draped his towel around his neck, subtly flashing his wedding band in the process.

As he accepted the surprised congratulations from his friends, he was glad he'd come tonight. He'd only done so, though, because Stevie had a meeting and he'd figured he might as well stick to his regular schedule.

She wasn't yet home when he let himself in. He dropped his keys in a little basket she used for that purpose and wiped his feet carefully on the mat leading in from the garage before bending down to greet Dusty with a pat.

Stevie kept her house impeccably neat. When he'd first met her, he'd have assumed she lived in cheery chaos. His own housekeeping skills were limited to keeping things mostly in their place and wielding a mop once a week or so, but he made sure not to make a mess here. Not that Stevie would have minded. As tidy as she was, she made her home a comfortable, welcoming place, and she didn't seem bothered by Dusty's toys that popped up all over the house, or the occasional scattered kibble or rare, but inevitable, hairballs. She wouldn't fret about kid's toys spread across the living room floor, either, he thought, picturing just that as he moved through the living room toward the bedroom.

He was freshly showered and dressed in a T-shirt and pajama pants when she arrived an hour later. She hung up her coat. "Sorry I'm so late. The meeting ran over. How was your evening?"

"Not bad. Sparred a couple of times. Won the second time. Got my butt handed to me in the first bout."

She laughed and moved to pat his cheek. "Someone beat up my hubby? Should I be incensed?"

Catching her hand, he leaned his head down to kiss her lingeringly. "I'll recover," he said when he released her.

Her cheeks looking a little flushed now, she cleared her throat. "Glad to hear it. Do you ever have spectators at monthly sparring things? I'd like to watch you sometime."

"Occasionally someone tags along, but we're not really performing for an audience. Just trying to stay in shape."

"Still. I'd like to see you being all manly and sexy."

He laughed in response to the teasing phrase she'd used before. "As long as you don't call me a 'cutie' in front of my opponents," he said, remembering the addition she'd tacked on last time.

Giggling, she moved toward the bedroom, looking

over her shoulder. "I'm sure they're already aware of that."

He lasted all of a full second before he gave in to that beckoning look and followed her.

Chapter Seven

Along with Jenny and Gavin, Stevie and Cole were invited to a Sunday potluck lunch in the sprawling home Tess shared with her fiancé, Scott Prince. The cozy gathering was a celebration of Stevie and Cole's new marriage, and a chance for Cole to meet the other men.

It was still too cold to lunch out on the patio, so they ate in the dining room. They lingered a long time over the meal of side dishes they'd all contributed and succulent short ribs Scott had cooked on his beloved fancy grill. There was no lull in the conversation, of course. Stevie and her girlfriends never had trouble filling a silence. The men were a little quieter at first—possibly because they didn't have much chance to speak—but she was glad that Cole was soon involved in conversations with them.

"They seem to be getting along well," Tess commented while she and Jenny and Stevie prepared coffee and scooped blackberry cobbler into bowls after lunch.

The men were outside admiring the barbecue kitchen that was Scott's pride and joy. Stevie could see Cole through the patio doors, and he looked relaxed and comfortable. Despite the cold, none of them seemed in a hurry to come back in. Maybe they were enjoying a few minutes of quiet out there, she thought with an understanding smile. But they came in eagerly after being summoned for dessert.

"Oh, wow, Jen, this is good," Scott said, attacking his cobbler with enthusiasm.

She beamed. "Thanks. It's my grandmother's recipe. We won't mention calories, since this is a celebration party."

"Speaking of which…" Tess stood and dashed from the room for a moment, returning shortly afterward with a couple of large, beautifully wrapped gifts that she placed in front of Stevie and Cole.

"This seems like a good time for you to open these," she said, her smile including both of them. "This one is from Jenny and Gavin and this one is from Scott and me."

Stevie gasped in pleasure. "Oh, how sweet."

Cole looked startled by the unexpected gifts. "It was nice, but you didn't have to—"

Stevie elbowed him teasingly into silence. "Hush, before they decide to take them back," she chided and reached out to open the nearest package.

Obviously, Jenny and Tess had shopped together because the gifts were coordinated—a gorgeous porcelain tea service and a matching set of dessert plates featuring the sage green that was Stevie's favorite color.

"I know they're a little feminine, but we figured you'd enjoy eating sweets and drinking tea from them," Jenny said to Cole.

"They're great," he assured her. "Thanks, everyone."

Gavin gave a rough laugh and held up his hands. "To be strictly honest, I didn't even know what we'd gotten. But congratulations, anyway. You're a lucky man."

"Yes," Cole agreed with a glance at Stevie. "I know."

"And," Jenny said, her eyes glowing, "our kids can grow up together, just as Stevie and I did. They'll probably think of themselves as cousins."

"Makes sense, with you and Stevie as close as sisters," her doting husband commented. He glanced at Cole then. "How are your diapering skills, Cole? As for me, I've got a lot to learn yet."

"Same here," Cole admitted with a faint smile. "But I'm looking forward to the experience."

Stevie was sure Gavin and Scott had been filled in on the details of her pregnancy. It pleased her that they were treating it with such equanimity. For Cole's sake, especially, she was relieved that there was no awkwardness in the discussion of impending parenthood.

"We've already started working on our nursery," Jenny said, reaching out to take Gavin's hand. "We know we have plenty of time yet, but there's quite a bit to do. With our busy schedules, we'll have to work on it whenever we get a little extra time. Fortunately, Gavin's very handy around the house. All that work he's done at his fishing cabin has given him a lot of carpentry experience."

"What about you, Stevie?" Tess asked. "Have you thought about your nursery yet?"

"Yes." She mentioned the bedroom she'd decided upon. Familiar with her house, everyone nodded in approval. "Cole and I are still working out details. We'd like to have a guest room, but I'm using the third bedroom for an office. Cole is having to use the office at his house next door, which is inconvenient and impractical. It's possible we'll sell both our houses and try to find one that will better accommodate our needs."

Scott frowned thoughtfully. "You have a great house—classic mid-50s bungalow. And the neighborhood is good. If you want to stay there, you should consider some renovations. You could remodel the attic into two decent-sized home offices with plenty of built-in storage. I have a few connections in residential work if you want to proceed. I could have my architect draw up a plan and an estimate for you."

Intrigued, Stevie glanced at Cole, who gave her a gesture that told her he considered this more her decision than his. She frowned, but smoothed the expression quickly. True, it was still technically her house, but a remodel like this would certainly affect him, too.

For some reason, she thought of that tense moment in the baby store in Branson, when she'd been so determined to assert her financial independence. Had that moment of obstinacy really been for his sake—or for her own? They'd never talked about the incident afterward. Had she gone too far with her insistence that she hadn't married him for monetary assistance? Had he taken away the message that she wanted him to be hands-off in other areas of their lives, as well? Their home—even this child? That hadn't been her intention at all. She'd have to find the right time to have that discussion with him, and she'd have to do a better job of expressing her concerns without hurting his male pride.

"I'd like to think about it," she said, looking at Scott again. "It's definitely a possibility and one I hadn't yet considered. Thanks for the suggestion."

"How long would a renovation like that take?" Cole

asked, and Stevie was pleased he seemed interested, at least.

"From plans to completion, maybe six, seven weeks, assuming everything goes smoothly."

"So it could be finished before August?"

Scott considered a moment, then shrugged lightly. "I should think so."

Cole nodded. "Definitely something to think about."

The conversation moved on, skipping from renovations and babies to wedding plans. Gavin was still on night shift rotation, so he had to leave not long afterward, and the party came to an end with hugs and kisses all around and promises to get together often. Stevie thought Jenny and Tess looked a bit more reassured about her marriage to Cole now that they'd spent more time with him, but she knew they still worried. They loved her. They wanted her to be happy. They wished for her what they'd found for themselves, even though she had assured them she was content with what she'd found.

She frowned. The word didn't feel quite right in her mind. Was "contentment" all she truly wanted with him? Or—she swallowed—was it the best she could expect?

A short while later, she and Cole walked into their home, placing their gifts on the kitchen counter to be put away later.

"Well?" Stevie said, reaching down to pick up Dusty and snuggle her beneath her chin, asking Cole, "You liked Scott and Gavin, huh?"

"Sure. They seem like great guys."

"Did I hear that you and Gavin have some mutual friends?"

"Yeah, through the gym and dojo. Not that big a surprise. For a medium-sized city, Little Rock's a small world in some ways. I'm sure Scott and I would find a mutual acquaintance or two if we put our heads to it hard enough."

"Probably." Feeling suddenly overwarm, she put down the cat and tugged off the oversized cardigan she'd worn over a black shirt and leggings. She pressed a hand to her middle. "I think maybe I ate a little too much today. Peanut's not used to so much good food at once."

Cole stepped toward her, searching her face. "Are you ill?"

She held him off with one raised hand. "No. Just a little unsettled, that's all."

"I'll make you some peppermint tea."

"That sounds good, but I can—" Too late. He was already headed for the stove.

Shaking her head, she went into the bedroom to hang up her sweater. She was tempted to put on her pj's and get comfortable since she had no intention of leaving the house again that day, but it was still a little early. Not even dinnertime yet. If Cole weren't there, she'd say the heck with the time and "jammie," anyway, but...

She growled as she realized the direction her thoughts had drifted. Why was she treating him like a guest in the home she'd thought of as his, too, only an hour or so earlier? If she wanted to wear pajamas before dinner, she should do so. She wasn't going to walk around in tatters, but she had some cute lounging clothes, and darn if she wasn't going to get comfortable in her own—in *their* own home.

"Your tea is ready." Cole stood in the doorway a few minutes later, watching her as she examined herself in the full-length mirror. "Are you okay?"

"Yes." She'd donned a long-sleeved purple top with purple and green plaid dorm pants and fuzzy pink socks. "I decided to get comfy for the evening. My clothes were feeling a little tight."

"Your tea is ready."

"What did you think about Scott's idea of renovating the attic?" she asked, following him to the kitchen.

He poured the tea and handed her one of the mugs. "Sounded promising. Now you'll just have to decide if you want to remodel and stay here or look elsewhere for more space."

"I do love this house," she said, gazing wistfully around the kitchen she'd poured her heart, soul and savings into.

"Then maybe you should consider Scott's suggestions."

Cupping her mug between her hands, she leaned back against the counter and studied him gravely. "I have one major concern about that plan."

"Oh? What's that?"

"You."

Taken by surprise, he lowered his mug with a little cough. "Me? Why?"

"I worry that as long as we live here, you'll think of yourself as a guest in my home. That's not what I want. Maybe if we sell both houses and invest in someplace new, it will feel like ours rather than mine."

"Stevie." Setting his mug on the counter, he rested a hand lightly on her shoulder. "I appreciate your concern, really. And I'll admit this is all taking some getting used to mentally. That's only natural. I'm already feeling more at home here. If we set up an office upstairs so I'm not running next door for most of the day, it'll feel even more like my place, too."

Running a fingertip around the rim of her cup, she eyed him through her lashes. "You really didn't mind moving in here rather than your house?"

He shrugged. "I like my house fine, but I have no particular emotional attachment to it. I've only lived there a year. You grew up in this one. I can sell my place and put some of the profit toward the upstairs remodel, or we can hang on to it as rental property, if we want to deal with the occasional annoyances of being landlords. Doesn't really matter to me."

He really didn't seem to have much of a connection to his house. To him, it was just a place to live and work, a roof over his head. Of course, he'd never shared that home with anyone but his cat. Would that have made a difference? Did he still have warm feelings about whatever home he'd shared with his late wife, or had he seen that place, too, as just basic shelter? Maybe it really didn't matter to him where they lived, and she could feel less conflicted about staying in this house she didn't want to leave.

"Okay, we'll look at the figures Scott works up for us," she said. "But we'll make sure there's plenty of room for you to work up there. I don't need much space, just a cubbyhole for a desk and computer and maybe some built-in shelves."

"You pretty much described all I need, as well. I think we'll get by just fine here."

Get by. He probably hadn't intended for that phrase to sound so lackluster. He'd simply been agreeing that Scott's idea had been a good one.

A workable plan for a growing family in a house she loved and that he considered adequate for their needs. What more could she possibly want?

* * *

They settled into more of a routine during the next three weeks. Every morning, Cole kissed her after breakfast and headed next door to work as she left for her midtown office or job sites. Most afternoons he visited his gym for an hour or so, then put in a couple hours more work before dinner. He insisted on helping her with food prep and cleanup and he did his share of housework. More than his share, perhaps, she thought with a shake of her head.

Unless one of them had an appointment, they spent most evenings at home. Sometimes they played board games, though Cole quickly despaired of teaching her the finer points of Japanese strategy games, for which she had little patience. Conversation was never a challenge. They chatted about work and friends and current events, about politics and religion and philosophy, about literature, music and hobbies they'd sampled over the years. They didn't always agree, but she found the workings of his mind fascinating, and he seemed to value her opinions in a respectful way that was rather new to her coming from the man in her life.

During those three weeks, they got to know each other in other ways, as well. Stevie was delighted by the increasing awareness that Cole was the best lover she'd ever known. In the bedroom, too, Cole respected her and encouraged her, making her feel beautiful and desirable and sensual. He didn't play emotional games or try to manipulate her; he simply stated what he liked and expected the same of her. He didn't use flowery words, of course. No cutesy nicknames. That was so not Cole. He merely murmured her name, and something about hearing it in his deep, rumbly voice affected her in a way no poetry ever had.

She told herself she should be more content than she'd ever been. But an annoying little voice deep inside her whispered that something was still missing. And it still seemed to have something to do with that word...*content*.

She wished she could say for certain how Cole felt. He appeared to be—she grimaced in response to the word that popped into her mind—content. But was that enough for him? For either of them?

Physically—well, she had no doubt that neither of them had complaints in that area. They were dynamite in bed. Their explosive chemistry had proven a delightful surprise for her, and he'd made it very clear he felt the same. But was he really happy with the way things were going for them otherwise? No secret regrets? They were both mature enough to understand the difference between physical attraction and true love. Was the life they were making for themselves anything at all like what he'd shared with Natasha?

As subtly as possible for her, she'd tried a couple of times to coax him to talk about his first marriage. After all, that had been a significant part of her husband's past. Yet every time she'd brought it up, he'd changed the subject. She'd gotten the message that he didn't want to talk about his late wife. Was it still too painful for him? She couldn't help wondering wistfully if she would ever measure up to his memories of Natasha. What worried her even more was that someday, even as generous and considerate as he'd been, she wouldn't be quite as satisfied with what Cole had left for her. Telling herself to stop being greedy and focus on gratitude instead, she pushed those concerns to the back of her mind each time they tried to creep forward.

She met her friends for lunch the third Tuesday in

March. As usual, they launched straight into conversation, catching up on everything that had happened since they'd last talked.

"So, anyway, I told Gavin that he absolutely had to back off or I'm going to lose my mind long before this baby ever arrives," Jenny said, continuing a diatribe to her sympathetic friends. "I told him to save all that helpful hovering for the last few weeks of the pregnancy when I'll be all bloated and surly and unable to get around easily. I don't want him burning out on caregiving this early in the process."

Tess laughed. "How did he react to that?"

"Oh, you know Gavin. He pouted for a while, then he apologized and promised he'd tone it down. I told him I thought it was sweet that he wants to take care of me, and I know he isn't sure what he's supposed to be doing at this early stage, but geez."

After Stevie and Tess laughed, Tess looked toward Stevie. "What about Cole? Is he prone to hovering?"

"No, that's not his style. He's just reliably there for me. He tells me occasionally to be careful, and he's made me assure him I won't hesitate to ask for anything I need, but he isn't a hoverer."

She was aware that both her best friends eyed her closely as she talked about her husband. She knew she'd been a bit circumspect in discussing her marriage with them. She didn't know why, exactly, because she'd been prone to share even intimate details of her previous romances. But Cole was a private man, and she respected his comfort zone too much to breach his trust.

"Okay, I just told you that Scott and I butted heads over something at work this morning, and Jen told us about her confrontation with Gavin last night," Tess recapped. "So what do you and Cole fuss about?"

Stevie blinked, then spread her hands. "Nothing."

Jenny snorted skeptically. "Nothing? Seriously? I think I know you better than that, Stevie."

She understood why Jenny would question her. It wasn't that she had a bad temper, but she wasn't one to hold back her feelings, either. She got mad, she expressed it, then she just as quickly forgave and moved on. The closest she'd come to quarreling with Cole had been when she'd snapped at him in the baby store on their honeymoon, she realized now. He hadn't gotten angry in return, and had seemed to go out of his way not to step on her toes since. She bit her lower lip. Was that a healthy thing?

"You said he's in Chicago this week?" Tess inquired.

Stevie heard her own little wistful sigh before she replied, "Yes. He left this morning. He'll be back Friday. He doesn't usually have to travel as much as he has the past couple of months, but there've been issues with a conversion to some sort of new data system that's totally beyond my comprehension."

Jenny toyed with her food, but her gaze was still focused on Stevie. "So you have the house to yourself again for a few days."

"Yes. I have to admit it already feels a little odd not to have him there." She laughed quietly. "Dusty isn't much of a conversationalist, though she is good company."

Jenny allowed the full measure of her concern to show on her face. "So you're happy with Cole?"

"I'm happy," she said firmly. "We're getting along very well and we're both looking forward to the baby. We love the plans Scott's architect drew up for our attic renovation and the estimate was very reasonable, so we're excited about moving forward with that, too."

Maybe "excited" wasn't the best adjective to describe Cole's satisfaction with the plan, but close enough, she decided. "We've agreed it will be better to stay at his place while the staircase construction is underway. Once we're settled again, we'll decide whether to sell or rent out his house."

"Sounds like you have your future all planned out," Tess remarked.

"As much as anyone can plan for the future."

"Do you think you and Cole will have more children?" Tess asked artlessly.

Stevie blinked, caught off-guard by the question that hadn't even occurred to her until now. "We haven't had this one yet," she said, resting a hand on the more noticeable bulge of her tummy.

"But you *are* sleeping together?" Jenny asked bluntly. "And by sleeping, of course, I mean—"

"Jen," Tess murmured, apparently deciding the questioning had gone just a bit too far with that one.

Jenny's expression was a mixture of apology and defiance. She spoke quietly, her words audible only to Stevie and Tess in their corner booth. "She understands why I'd ask. We've known each other since we were kids, right, Stevie? I knew the day you had your first period. The day you got your first of several broken hearts. I know you lost your virginity after senior prom to the first of those heartbreakers. You knew when Gavin became my first, something you recognized the minute I walked into our dorm room afterward. I'm fully aware this is none of my business. You can tell me to jump into a lake and I won't get mad, because you have every right to do so. But you know I love you, and I worry about you. And you have to admit you've never been shy about expressing your opinions when you were concerned about me."

There was no way Stevie could hold out against that heartfelt speech. For one thing, every word of it was true.

She drew a deep, steadying breath. "Cole and I married for the sake of this child neither of us was expecting but both of us want," she said, paraphrasing something he'd once said to her. "And yes, it is a real marriage in every way. It's a win-win-win situation. The baby gets a father, I get a partner in raising the child and Cole gets a family. It's what we both want. Thank you for caring. I love you both, and I'm glad all of us are happy now. I'm looking forward to raising our kids together, backyard barbecues and birthday parties, being eccentric old lady friends who get together and brag about our grandchildren. I know I didn't go about this marriage in a typical manner...but when have I ever been typical?"

Her eyes suspiciously liquid, Jenny managed a watery smile. "Never. And I wouldn't change a thing about you."

"That goes both ways," Stevie said gruffly, returning the smile.

"So could I ask just one more question?"

Stevie growled humorously, wondering when she and Jenny had swapped personalities. This sounded exactly like a conversation they'd have had in the past, only with roles reversed. "What the hell. Ask."

"Is there any chance you're falling in love with Cole?"

"I—" Stevie took a quick sip of her water to loosen her suddenly tight throat. "Cole is a sweet, kind, very special man. Of course I love him."

"I asked if you're *in* love with him. But never mind."

Jenny shook her head, her expression genuinely apologetic now. "You're right, Stevie, I'm stepping way over the line here. Let's just change the subject, okay? It's almost time for us all to get back to work, anyway."

Stevie nodded gratefully.

"For what it's worth, I think Cole knows how lucky he is," Tess said, speaking quickly to defuse the tension before they moved on. "He hardly took his eyes off you when we gathered at our house. I bet he's missing you while he's away."

She hoped he did miss her a little, Stevie thought as she sat on the couch later that evening, the dozing cat curled in her lap. Funny how quiet and empty the house seemed now without him in it, especially considering he wasn't one to make much noise when he was there. It was just that she'd become accustomed to his quiet presence. His warmth beside her in her bed at night. And she missed him.

Dusty mewed and looked up at her. Stevie scratched the cat's ears in the way she'd seen Cole do numerous times, and the cat purred with pleasure.

"You miss him, too, don't you?" she asked the tabby, who arched her neck for better access.

"I do love him, of course. We've had such a special friendship. It meant a great deal to me, even before we took this step."

Dusty sneezed.

"And would it really be such a bad thing if I do fall in love with my husband? Seems to me that would be something to be desired. And hardly a risk for heartbreak since we're already married and we plan to stay together."

No heartbreak from a breakup, anyway, she couldn't help adding silently, looking away from the unconcerned cat. But how would it feel to realize she was head over heels in love with a man who was merely fond of her? How much would it hurt to know that while she was sitting here missing him so much, he'd hardly given her a thought?

Her phone rang and she jumped, startling the cat who leapt down to the floor. Seeing Cole's number on her screen, she cleared her throat before answering. "How's Chicago?"

"Let's just say I'm looking forward to being home."

"Good. Dusty and I miss you," she said lightly.

"I miss you guys, too. How are things there?"

It was hardly a yearning declaration, but she'd take it. "Everything's fine. I had a few complications come up with Pepper Rose's kitchen redesign, but I think we've taken care of them."

"Nothing major?"

"Not in this case. Just a frustrating back order situation. It'll work out."

"Good. How's Peanut?"

"Growing. I had to change my mind about an outfit this morning because I couldn't button the shirt. By the way, I'd almost forgotten that I have a doctor's appointment next week. Would you like to go with me?"

"Absolutely." He sounded pleased that she'd asked.

"Okay, then. I'll introduce you to my doctor. You'll like her."

"I'm sure I will. Didn't you mention you were having lunch with Tess and Jenny today?"

"Yes, I did. They send their regards."

"So you had a good visit?"

"Yes, it was very nice."

He seemed to sense something beneath her words,

proving once again that Cole was just a little too perceptive when it came to her. "Is anything wrong?"

"I'm just a little tired, I guess. Long day."

"I'll let you rest. But if you fall asleep on the couch,
you'll have to depend on Dusty to wake you to go to
bed."

She laughed. "I'll let her know. Good night, Cole."

"'Night, Stevie."

He disconnected without further delay.

She looked at the silent phone. "Hurry home," she
said.

The aroma of spices and peppers greeted Cole when
he walked into the house early Friday evening. Stevie
had ordered him not to eat at the airport. Judging by
the scents and the clues on the kitchen counter, she'd
prepared Tex-Mex. His stomach was already growling
in response. She wasn't in the kitchen, so he moved toward the doorway to find her.

Dusty appeared and meowed in welcome. Setting
down his bag, he bent to greet her, then picked up his
bag again and headed for the doorway. He found Stevie
in the bedroom, fluffing her hair at the mirror, seemingly unaware he was home yet. Was she primping for
his arrival? The possibility pleased him, for some reason. Not that she needed enhancement. She wore something blue and floaty over black leggings with black
slippers. Nearly the same color as her eyes, her blouse
draped appealingly over her full bust and fell loosely
to her hips, almost but not quite concealing the little
bulge at her middle.

She looked beautiful.

Sensing his presence, she turned to look his way. Her

face lit up, her brilliant blue eyes glowing with pleasure. "Cole! You're home."

She launched herself at him and he dropped his bag with a laugh to catch her. His lips found hers in a kiss that made him all but forget his hunger for food.

As he'd expected, it felt damned good to be welcomed home this way, he thought as Dusty wound around their ankles. He never wanted to go back to always returning to a dark, quiet house.

Yet he, better than most people, knew how capricious life could be, how quickly circumstances could change. His arms tightened reflexively around Stevie, as if he could keep her safe and satisfied simply by holding her close.

Chapter Eight

"Anyway, we finally got the materials for Pepper's backsplash, and the plumber finally got the pipes in the right place. Honestly, that man can be so dense sometimes. Now that that job is moving along, the Blankenship remodel is about to make me pull my hair out. If Mindy changes her mind one more time about where she wants her refrigerator, I'm going to give her deposit back and tell her to draw up her own plans. Or tell her good luck finding someone to help her make a decision that comes with a guarantee of one hundred percent long-term satisfaction, which is more than I can seem to do for a woman who changes her vision of what she wants every morning when she wakes up. Heck, she changes her mind half a dozen times before lunch every day! Honestly, Cole, sometimes I wonder—"

He cleared his throat to break into the animated monologue. "Excuse me, Stevie, I'm paying attention to what you're saying, but is there any more of that salsa?"

She was startled into momentary silence before bursting into a peal of rueful laughter. "Poor Cole. I've been talking your ears off, haven't I? I guess I had a lot of words saved up for you. Yes, there's more salsa in the fridge. I'll—"

"Sit," he said when she started to rise. "I'll get it. Go on with what you were saying. Do you think you'll ever be able to please Mrs. Blankenship?"

"I'm sure I will. Maybe. With luck."

After returning to the table, he leaned down to brush a kiss at the corner of her mouth, his lips warm and spicy against her skin. She all but shivered in response to his touch. It seemed like more than a mere few days since she'd felt it.

He gave her shoulder a little squeeze before releasing her to take his seat. "I like hearing your stories. And knowing that maybe you missed me a little while I was away."

"More than a little." She hoped her smile looked natural. "Like that old song says, I've grown accustomed to your face."

He laughed, and as always the sound pleased her. "I'm glad." He dipped a tortilla chip into the spicy homemade salsa. "I've gotten pretty accustomed to yours, too. So, what's the next step with Mrs. Blankenship?"

As far as romantic exchanges went, that one had hardly been the most lyrical she'd ever participated in. Yet still she'd taken it to heart. Which only showed how little it took to please her when it came to Cole. What, exactly, did that say about her growing feelings for him? And how could she tell if he felt the same when he kept his emotions so very well concealed behind that sexy, unrevealing smile?

A couple hours later she watched with a thrill of anticipation as he emerged from the master bathroom and into the bedroom where she waited for him. She'd turned off the overhead light, leaving the room lit only by the lamp on the nightstand. Cole's bare chest gleamed in that soft glow as he approached the bed wearing only boxer shorts. His broad shoulders and firm muscles were outlined by shadows, and his dark eyes glittered like polished onyx as he studied her with a smile.

He turned out the light before climbing in beside her, plunging the room into darkness but leaving that image of him very clear in her mind. She folded herself into his eager arms, her mouth meeting his in a kiss that clearly established how much she'd missed him in their bed as well as at their dinner table. And though Cole wasn't one to express himself with words, he was breathtakingly efficient at conveying with his hands and lips how pleased he was to be back.

He trailed a string of openmouthed kisses from her mouth to her temple, from the soft indention behind her ear to the pulsing hollow of her throat. His big, warm hand cupped her left breast through her thin nightgown, his thumb rotating lazily over the nipple. She arched in reaction.

"Too sensitive?" he asked in a low rumble, lifting his thumb.

Catching his hand, she pressed it down again. "Feels good," she murmured, tangling her smooth legs with his longer, hair-roughened limbs.

He lowered his head, tugging the deep neckline of the gown out of the way so his mouth could find that achingly distended nub. With exquisite tenderness, he caressed it with his lips and with strokes of his tongue drew it into his mouth, then released it and soothed it with a rub of his closed mouth before he turned his attention to its jealous twin. His hand slid down her side, appreciatively shaping her changing form before finding the hem of her gown and slipping beneath it to stroke the heated depths he discovered there.

She gasped and plunged her hands into his hair. His thick, springy, beautiful hair. She held his head at her breasts, parted her legs to allow him full access to her secrets, lifted herself against him in a way that made it very clear how much she wanted him. She'd never been shy about her sexuality, but Cole had a talent for taking her to heights of sensation she'd never imagined, and she was impatient to find out just how high they could climb together.

When the last shred of patience evaporated, she shoved at his shoulders until he tumbled laughing on his bed against the pillows. Boxers and nightgown hit the floor and she straddled him, bracing herself with her hands on his solid shoulders. Her eyes had adjusted to the darkness now and she could just see him there against the white linens, grinning up at her with a flash of white teeth that gave her a glimpse of the warrior hidden deep inside this self-proclaimed computer nerd. And as always, that tantalizing peek made her even hungrier for more.

His hands on her hips, her hair falling around them, their moans and murmurs blending as their bodies merged, they reached that dazzling summit together, clinging there for as long as they could draw it out before they plunged almost simultaneously over the edge into a maelstrom of mindless sensation. Collapsing into his strong arms afterward, she wasn't sure she'd ever catch another full breath or form another coherent sentence, but at the moment, she just didn't care.

She was so glad to have him back home.

The doctor's appointment the following Monday went well. With the exception of slightly elevated blood pressure, Stevie was pronounced healthy, as was the baby. Though she'd been seeing the doctor only once a month until then, she was instructed to come in every other week from that point on. Dr. Prescott didn't seem overly concerned about the blood pressure reading, but she said they should monitor it closely just to be on the safe side. Stevie didn't argue.

"You were right," Cole said as he drove them away from the appointment. "I liked your doctor very much."

"I thought you would. She's great."

He was frowning a little when he asked, "Do you have a history of high blood pressure?"

"No. But it's okay. She said it's probably nothing to worry about, remember? It wasn't much higher than usual. How cool was it when she said those funny little feelings I've noticed during the past week are probably the baby kicking? I mean, I thought it could be, but they were just little flutters, not like real kicks yet, so I wasn't completely sure. But she said it's very likely that's what I'm feeling and it should start getting strong and it won't be long until you'll be able to feel it from the outside. And they're doing the next ultrasound in just four more weeks and we should be able to tell the gender by then so we can start narrowing down our list of names and it's all just so exciting."

He chuckled and she realized she'd let her enthusiasm carry her away for the moment. "Sorry. I know you heard her say all of that. I'm just glad the checkup went well. I get nervous every time beforehand."

"I noticed," he said, and she made a little face as she remembered how restless she'd been that morning, pacing through the house and checking the clock every few minutes until it was time to leave. "You were too nervous to eat much this morning. Want to stop for a bite somewhere?"

She tilted her head in consideration, then nodded. "Actually, I'm starving. You know what sounds good? Sushi."

"Aren't you supposed to avoid— "

"I know, raw fish is a bad idea in pregnancy. So maybe I'll just have udon noodles with chicken. That's sort of like sushi, right?"

He laughed. "That's nothing like sushi, other than being from the same country, but okay. We'll find udon noodles. Whatever you want."

Whatever you want. He said those words a lot, she mused, thoughtfully twisting a lock of hair. Sometimes she still felt as if their relationship was very uneven, as though she were the one getting most of the benefits while he was the one doing the bulk of the giving. That was still hard for her to get used to.

Someday, she promised herself, she'd find a way to do something special for Cole, other than preparing good meals for him and trying to make a nice home with him.

They chose to dine at a small Asian fusion chain restaurant located in a midtown shopping center. It was a popular destination for workday lunch crowds, and though it was a bit later than the work rush, the place was still busy. They'd just spotted an available two-top and Cole had pulled out a chair for Stevie when a woman said his name.

"Cole? I thought that was you."

The woman was tall and fit, her skin lightly tanned and her brown hair sun-streaked as if she spent a lot of time outdoors. Something about the way she smiled at Cole made Stevie's feminine nerve endings tingle in awareness. She had to resist an urge to take a step closer to him. She'd never in her life been the possessive or jealous type. She wondered in bewilderment if pregnancy hormones were messing with her again.

"Oh, hi, Jessica. Nice to see you," Cole said cordially, his hands still on the back of the chair.

"Sorry you didn't make it for sparring last week," she commented. "We missed you there."

"I was out of town on business. I'll try to make it next time. Oh, uh, Jessica Lopez, this is my wife, Stevie."

Stevie noted that the other woman's gaze slid down to her little baby bump, paused there a moment, then lifted back to her face. Jessica definitely had had a little crush on Cole, and was fully resigned now that nothing would ever come of it.

Because Stevie couldn't blame any woman for being drawn to Cole, she added a bit more warmth to her voice when she said, "It's very nice to meet you."

"Yeah, you, too. See you, Cole."

Cole motioned Stevie into the chair he still held for her. Drinks were self-serve at this ultracasual place, so he asked what she wanted then went to fetch it while she thought about the little encounter with Jessica.

She doubted Jessica was the only woman who'd been drawn to Cole during the past few years. She was sure he met nice women at his gym, on his business trips, in other everyday pursuits. He'd said he liked being married, but he'd apparently made no effort to court any-one during the five years he'd been single, not until her own situation had spurred him into action. So had he really been satisfied living on his own—or had no one lived up to his memories?

He'd implied on their wedding night that he'd been attracted to her for a while, though he'd done a good job of masking it during their year of platonic friend-ship. Would he ever have acted on that attraction had it not been for her pregnancy? Could she take encourage-ment in the fact that he'd chosen to finally change his single status for her, even though it had taken a fairly significant development to prod him into it?

He returned with their drinks and a couple of for-tune cookies for after the meal. Their food arrived at almost the same time. Stevie picked up her chopsticks and dug in enthusiastically, making Cole chuckle at her eagerness. "How is it?"

"It's not sushi, but it's good, anyway."

He laughed and picked up his own chopsticks. Maybe for Cole, what they had was all he needed.

Maybe she should take a lesson from him.

They were able to start on the renovations the Thurs-day after the doctor's appointment. Spring was trying its best to shoulder winter out of the way, leading to noisy thunderstorms and one night of severe weather warn-ings. Considering they lived in the middle of "tornado alley," they'd decided to install a safe room in the ga-rage while they were remodeling. The addition would add a week to the process but would provide a safe place for their little family to gather in dangerous weather. The shelter was Cole's idea initially, but Stevie heart-ily agreed. She'd spent too many nights in her lifetime huddling in a hallway or bathroom waiting for the tornado sirens to stop wailing.

She got a little taste of how he must have felt for the past six weeks when they moved into his house to avoid the mess created by the staircase reconstruction in her hallway. She didn't know where everything was, she bumped her shins on the furniture when the lights were off, the mattress on his bed felt different and her clothes were crowded into the extra space he made for her. It was a nice house, but it wasn't home. Maybe it was a good thing Cole didn't get attached to houses and possessions, she reflected ruefully. He'd adjusted much more easily to being surrounded by someone else's things than she would have. Even Dusty seemed to handle displacement better!

"When we get settled back into our house," she said as she and Cole sat at the kitchen table for dinner the second night, "we need to integrate your things there more. Are there any special pieces of furniture you want to move over? I'm sure we can make a place for anything you'd like to keep."

He glanced around as if the option had never occurred to him. "I'll keep my desk and office chair, of course. But all my work stuff will fit into the new office."

"What about any other furniture you particularly like?" He didn't possess more than the basics, and she hadn't noticed anything that looked as though it might be an heirloom, but maybe there was something that had sentimental attachment to him.

"Not really, no. Your stuff is nicer. We can have a tag sale with mine or rent the house furnished."

"You don't have any mementos from childhood or

college stashed in boxes somewhere? Things you want to keep?"

"I have a box in my closet with a few things like that," he said, slicing into the smothered pork chop she'd cooked for him. "It's not very big. I'll keep it in the closet of the new office."

She suspected those private treasures were things that had belonged to Natasha. She certainly didn't mind him hanging on to them. She would never be so petty that she would want him to forget his first wife or the few years he'd been allowed with her. It occurred to her that she'd never even seen a photograph of Natasha. Cole kept no framed photos out for display.

Had there been passion in his marriage? Had he and Natasha ever lost their tempers or even quarreled? He'd said she was very ill for some time. Had forewarning eased his loss, or had the grief been raw and devastating? Did it still tear at him sometimes, or had he packed those emotions away with that box in his closet?

"Stevie?" She glanced up to find him watching her quizzically from the other side of the table. "What's wrong? Are you feeling okay?"

She smiled reassuringly. "I'm fine. Just thinking about all we have to do during the next few weeks."

"Oh." That seemed to satisfy him. "Don't worry, it'll get done. I've got some free time tomorrow. Thought I'd work in the nursery while the crew's dealing with the staircase."

He'd volunteered to take care of emptying the small bedroom in preparation for the new nursery furniture they'd ordered. The walls had a few dents and nail holes to patch and the trim needed to be taped off before he could apply the rich cream color she'd chosen for the walls.

"Isn't there anything I can do for you here?" she asked. "Things I can pack or sort or something? I want to help as much as possible with this transition."

Finishing his dinner, he carried his dishes to the sink, collecting hers on the way. "I guess you could sort my closet some if you get bored. It's been a while since I've been through my wardrobe and I suspect some of the stuff in there needs to go straight into a donations bin."

From what she'd seen, his wardrobe consisted mostly of pullovers and jeans for working at home, with a couple of sport coats and dress shirts and slacks—and a few of the hated ties, she thought with a smile. "I'll look through your things and make a pile of items that could be questionable, though I'd never get rid of anything without checking with you."

He shrugged. "Wouldn't bother me. If you'd be embarrassed to be seen with me wearing anything you find in there, toss it."

"I'd never be embarrassed to be seen with you," she assured him, rising to refill her water glass.

"Oh, yeah? Not even if I do this?" He mugged a classic horror-movie-Igor pose, hunching a shoulder, dragging an arm, making a silly face.

Delighted with his rare lapse into absurdity, she gave a peal of laughter and tousled his hair. "Not even then. You're such a cutie."

Growling, he straightened and caught her in his arms. "There's that word again. I keep telling you, I'd rather you see me as manly and sexy."

He never forgot anything, she thought with another laugh. Wrapping her arms around his neck, she went up on tiptoes and brushed a kiss over his smiling mouth. "What a coincidence," she murmured. "That's exactly the way I see you. Most of the time."

Chuckling, he drew her into a heated kiss that definitely made this one of those times.

The first Sunday in April was Easter, and the day dawned clear and pleasantly moderate. Stevie dressed for church in a shades-of-purple graphic print dress, then checked her reflection. She was quite obviously pregnant now and made no effort to hide it. Actually, it was a relief that she was blossoming so quickly, as it meant her little Peanut was growing and thriving. The baby's movements were more frequent and noticeable now and she looked forward to Cole feeling the baby kick for the first time.

Everything seemed to be going so well that she was almost afraid she'd do something to jinx her good fortune. She wasn't used to feeling so relaxed in a relationship. She didn't have to walk on eggshells around Cole's ego, didn't have to second-guess her decisions or worry about plans being canceled last-minute or agreements being carelessly broken. When Cole said he'd do something or be somewhere, she could place a sizable bet on it.

She slid her feet into low-heeled shoes, her thoughts still focused on her marriage. She had to admit that so far it was going even better than she'd imagined it would the day they'd exchanged their vows. She wouldn't change a thing about their relationship. Except, perhaps...

No. Stop this, Stevie, before you jinx it, after all.

Ironically enough, she was aware that her biggest concern about her marriage was that it was too pleasant. And that Cole seemed to be trying too hard to keep it that way.

She'd never seen Cole come even close to losing control of his emotions, she thought, twisting a strand of hair. Her own had always been so close to the surface that she couldn't imagine how he managed. He was certainly passionate here in the bedroom, but even then his lovemaking always focused as much on her pleasure as his. She'd seen irritation—with his father, with annoying business associates—but never temper. Was it because he didn't feel things as intensely as she did, or had his childhood with a critical and emotionally distant father convinced Cole that a "real man" didn't acknowledge vulnerability?

Wouldn't it be only natural for him to get mad once in a while? Was it healthy, either emotionally or physically, for him to suppress anger if he felt it? Jenny and Tess certainly spatted occasionally with their guys, yet there was no doubt they were deeply in love and blissfully happy.

In love. She winced at the phrase. She wasn't comparing her relationship with those of her friends, of course. She and Cole had come at this with different needs than theirs. She simply wanted to make sure all his needs were being fulfilled. He was certainly taking care of hers.

"Stevie?"

In response to his voice from the doorway, she roused from her thoughts and turned toward him with a bright smile. "I'm ready."

Something about his expression made her stop and tilt her head to study him more closely. He looked great in the jacket and tie he'd donned for the holiday. But one hand was hidden behind his back and his face was as close to sheepish as she'd ever seen it.

"What is it?" she asked curiously. "Have you changed

your mind about going to church with me? Because that's certainly—"

"No, I want to go. I just —" Shaking his head a little, he brought his hand around. "I know it's a little silly, but I thought you might like this."

A little green wicker basket decorated with a green-and-white gingham bow dangled from his big fingers. Within the basket, a white stuffed bunny with floppy ears, big feet and an adorably sweet face sat on top of an assortment of her favorite specialty chocolates.

Stevie found it suddenly difficult to talk around a hard lump in her throat. Still, she managed to ask, "You brought me an Easter basket?"

"Yes. With your house all torn up and your schedule disrupted, I thought you'd like a little treat for Easter. I know you like these chocolates, so…"

His uncharacteristically self-conscious words faded into silence, leaving him looking almost shy as he held out the little basket to her. Stevie blinked back a film of tears when she accepted it from him. If she burst into sobs over his gesture, she was sure he would blame it on pregnancy hormones, and he would probably be right, for the most part. But it really was so sweet that her heart ached a bit.

"Can you see it?" Holding a cold metal wand pressed to Stevie's tummy, the sonographer looked with an indulgent smile from Stevie on the bed to Cole standing beside her. "Do you need me to show you?"

As curious as Cole was about what he'd see on the monitor, he was unable for a moment to tear his gaze away from Stevie's face. Her eyes looked bigger and bluer than ever, her beautiful mouth was curved into a smile of such joy he felt his throat tighten in response.

She was beautiful. And she was his, he thought with a surge of utterly male satisfaction.

She looked quickly from the screen to him and then back again. Her voice was breathy with excitement when she asked, "That's— It's a boy, right? That's a boy?"

The sonographer laughed, obviously enjoying her job no matter how many times she'd watched this reveal. "Yes, it's a boy. And he looks very healthy. Congratulations."

Stevie looked at Cole again with an expression radiant with wonder. "A boy, Cole. We're having a boy!"

He squeezed her hand, then impulsively raised it to his lips. Her fingers curled tightly around his. A hard knot formed in his throat when he looked back at the monitor with a knot in his throat.

A boy. For some reason, he'd been absolutely certain that Stevie was having a girl. As the past few weeks had swept by in a daze of work, construction, plans and commitments, the image had grown stronger in his mind of a little blonde girl with big blue eyes and a dimpled smile, a tiny clone of Stevie. He was very comfortable picturing himself as the father of that little girl. Helping her learn to walk. Holding her steady as she rode her first bike. Showing her constellations and planets, bugs and microbes. Teaching her how to drive, scowling off would-be suitors, maybe someday walking her down the aisle as no one had been there to do for Stevie. But a boy...

He studied the face in the ultrasound image, wondering if this little guy would have Stevie's curly hair and blue eyes. Looks didn't matter so much to him. He was more concerned with overcoming his own complex father-son issues and forming a bond with this boy. And for the first time in weeks, he was beset by doubts of his qualifications for the job.

"So now we're going to have to decide on a boy's name," Stevie announced happily when they were buckled into the car and he drove out of the clinic parking lot. "I've got a list started, but it has like fifty names on it already and every time I think I've narrowed it down a little I hear another name that's interesting enough to add to the list, so it's just getting longer instead of shorter. I've been keeping the nursery as neutral as possible with the classic children's tales artwork and the sage-and-cream color scheme, so nothing changes there, but now we can buy a few outfits because as much as I believe in equality, I just can't put a little boy in a lacy dress. I think in some ways I always knew he was a boy, even back when I first started calling him Peanut, which of course I won't do after we choose a name because heaven knows he wouldn't want that nickname to stick."

"No, he probably—"

"I have to text Jenny and Tess. I told them I'd let them know as soon as we left the clinic. They're almost as excited as we are to find out. And my mom and my brother want to know as soon as possible and I know your mother is eager to hear the news, so we'll have to make lots of calls and texts this evening. What about your dad? Are you going to call him?"

Cole's fingers tightened around the steering wheel. "Probably not."

She squirmed around in her seat to face him, surprise breaking into her excitement-fueled chattering. "You don't think he'd want to know the baby's gender?"

"Who knows with my dad?"

"You have told him I'm pregnant, haven't you?"

He cleared his throat. "I've only talked to him once

since we dropped by there in February, just for a routine six-week check to see how he's doing. The subject didn't come up."

There was a moment of shocked silence, and then her snort made her exasperation quite clear. "Honestly, Cole, you're almost as stubborn as he is. I know your dad was hard on you with his strict, narrow definition of masculinity, but has it occurred to you that maybe the prospect of being a grandfather would soften him up a little? That happens, you know, even with grumpy old men. It should especially please him that he'll have a grandson."

"So he can browbeat the boy the way he did me? Sigh at him when he cries or scowl at him if he doesn't want to tramp through the woods to kill a deer? I'm not going to let those things happen to this kid."

"We'd never let him do that. But if we establish clear boundaries and your dad follows them, maybe it would be good for both of them. I never knew my paternal grandfather and my mother's dad died when I was too young to remember him, but I always wished I had a grandpa if I couldn't have a dad. You and I could give our son both. You said you were close with your grandfather, and I'm sure he was pretty old-fashioned, too."

"He was," Cole conceded, thinking back to his hardworking, cattle farmer Pops. "He was strict, gave me plenty of rules and chores, but he wasn't as hard to please as my dad. Pops and I got along pretty well for the most part."

"And how was his relationship with his son?"

"Strained," Cole admitted slowly. "He got along better with his younger son, my uncle Bob. Pops didn't approve of Dad's marriage to my mother—rightly so, as it turned out—and he wasn't a fan of the way they kept putting me in the middle of their fights. He wasn't tactful with my father about his opinions, and Dad never took criticism well."

"Maybe your dad will find a soft spot for this little boy. Shouldn't we at least try to find out?"

"I'll think about it," he conceded grudgingly. "But frankly I'm tired of being the one to do all the reaching out. Dad knows my number. Wouldn't hurt him to call me every once in a while just to see if I'm still alive."

He shook his head before she could argue more. "Let's not talk about Dad now. This is too special a day. Why don't we celebrate this news by stopping by the baby store and picking up some more things for the kid? We're still looking for a stroller, right? Have you decided whether you want a three-wheel or four-wheel model?"

They'd done hours of research together on nearly everything they'd purchased to this point, reading all the safety records and brand comparisons they could find. He was pleased that Stevie wanted his opinions. Granted, he didn't know much about baby stuff, but he was damned good at research.

Stevie was enthused about shopping for the baby now that she knew more about him, and Cole was glad he'd made the suggestion. It was a sunny, warm spring day. He and Stevie had both been working so hard lately that it was nice to have a couple of daylight hours just to relax together. Maybe he'd talk her into a milkshake, which probably wouldn't be hard. She had a notorious weakness for chocolate milkshakes, and couldn't imagine why anyone—specifically, he—would want to ruin a perfectly good cup of ice cream with chunks of pineapple.

He was glad to see her happily chattering and laughing, so excited about learning more about the baby who'd be joining them in just over three months. She'd been a little more subdued than usual for the past few weeks—since Easter, really. He blamed it on all the turmoil in their lives. Stevie was accustomed to construction snafus and delays on her design jobs, but having the same things going on in her own home was more stressful, especially combined with the emotional roller coaster of pregnancy.

It still bemused him that she had such a strong attachment to her house. The place was certainly adequate for their needs, increasingly so as the attic renovation and storm shelter came closer to being finished, but he figured they'd have been able to find plenty of other houses just as functional. Maybe it was because he'd been shuttled so often from house to house as a kid that he didn't have as strong a sense of "home" as she did. For him, home was now wherever Stevie was. Didn't matter much where that happened to be. At least he had the satisfaction of knowing she missed him now when he wasn't in her beloved house with her.

"Are you sure you'll be okay when I'm away next week?" he asked as he parked in front of the baby store. "I can always try to change the meetings to conference calls if you—"

"Cole," she interrupted with a laugh and an affectionate pat on his arm. "You're starting to sound like Gavin. I'll be fine for a few days on my own, I promise."

He regretted missing next week's doctor's appointment, but this trip was rather important. He'd already made it clear to all involved that he wouldn't be traveling for a couple months after the baby arrived, so he was trying to take care of some things ahead of time. "You'll let me know if your blood pressure has gone up again? You'll tell the doctor you've had a couple of headaches in the past week?"

"Both of which occurred when I got busy and forgot to eat lunch on time," she reminded him. "Totally my fault. And I've been paying more attention to my schedule now that you set my phone to nag me about lunchtime. Haven't had a headache since. And my blood pressure has been stable the last two visits, so I think you can stop worrying about that, too."

He nodded slowly as he opened his door. Her blood pressure hadn't gone back down to prepregnancy levels, but it wasn't rising, either, so he guessed that was good. But that wouldn't stop him from worrying. Nothing would.

Chapter Nine

It was almost five p.m. when Stevie parked in front of McKellar Auto Service on the following Wednesday afternoon. She'd made the drive on one of her rash impulses and she was absolutely certain her husband would not approve had he known about it. But he was out of town, and she'd fought the urge as long as she could before heading north when she'd left a kitchen remodel job an hour earlier.

She might finally see her husband angry after this, she thought wryly as she climbed out of her car. But she'd been trying to think of something important to do for Cole ever since they'd gotten married. She hoped the result of this reckless mission would be worth incurring his initial anger.

There was more activity around the place than during her last brief visit, though she could tell it was nearing closing time. Several of the bay doors were open and she could see both mechanics and customers milling inside. Perhaps this hadn't been the best time to come by. Would Jim find her visit more intrusive than welcome?

She let herself into the door marked Office, finding only one person inside the cramped room. The broad-hipped, plain-faced woman at the paper-cluttered desk appeared to be about the same age as Jim. She wore a flowered T-shirt, faded jeans and sneakers, and her gray-streaked dishwater blond hair was tied back in a low ponytail. Was this Jim's wife?

"What can I do for you?" the woman asked in a broad country drawl. "Are you picking up a car?"

"Actually, I'd like to see Mr. McKellar, if he can spare just a few minutes."

The woman eyed her through red plastic-framed glasses. "Can I say who's calling?"

"I'm his daughter-in-law. My name is Stevie."

The older woman walked slowly around the end of the counter-styled desk. "You're Cole's wife?"

"Yes."

"I'm Peggy. Cole's stepmama." She directed a look at Stevie's middle, then glanced back up at her face. "Nice to meet you. I was sorry I missed you when you stopped by before."

So at least Jim had mentioned their visit. "It's very nice to meet you, too, Mrs. McKellar," she said warmly.

"Call me Peggy. Nothing's wrong with Cole, is there? He's okay?"

"Cole's fine. He's out of state on a business trip but he'll be back in a couple of days."

Peggy's eyebrows rose. "Does he know you're here?"

Making a little face, Stevie shook her head. "No."

"I'll get Jim. Move that parts catalog and sit in that chair if you need to take a load off your feet."

"I'm fine, thank you. I can't stay long."

Perhaps five minutes passed before Jim stepped in, closing the door behind him. He was wiping his hands on a shop towel, something Stevie now suspected was a habit to keep him from having to shake hands. She didn't bother to offer hers this time, though she gave him her most winning smile. "Hi, Mr. McKellar. It's good to see you again."

He nodded curtly. "What can I do for you?"

She felt her smile dim a little. To be honest, she was so accustomed to rather easily disarming people that she was a little startled Jim was not particularly receptive to her. "I just wanted a few words with you, if you have a couple of minutes."

"Did Cole send you?"

"No. He's away on a business trip. He doesn't know I'm here. It was sort of an impulsive visit."

"Hmph." Jim swept her with a look. "When are you due?"

"Early August. It's a boy. I thought you'd like to know."

The math was simple enough. He grunted, his face showing no particular emotional reaction to the news that he would have a grandson. Was he really so cold, or was he even better than his son at masking his thoughts?

"So that explains the quickie marriage. One of them 'have to' situations, huh?"

"No one 'has to' get married these days, Mr. McKellar. Cole and I chose to marry." For purposes that were none of his business, she added silently.

He shrugged. "I understand he makes good money doing whatever it is he does with computers."

For a moment she didn't follow him. The comment seemed to be a non sequitur. When it suddenly occurred to her what he was suggesting, she drew back with a frown. "I certainly didn't 'trap' Cole into marriage, if that's what you're implying."

Jim shook his head. Apparently her words had left him unconvinced. "That boy has always been a sucker for a woman in trouble. He married that last girl knowing she was likely going to die, but she didn't have anyone else to care for her at the time, coming from the worthless family she had. I didn't see any reason for him to put himself through that, but he never would listen to my advice. I know he went into debt paying her medical bills. Not that he ever asked for a penny from me, I'll give him that. So if you think he's got a bunch of money stashed away somewhere, I'd imagine you're wrong."

"Mr. McKellar—"

Either he didn't notice the signs of her mounting temper or he waved them off as insignificant. "And don't think you're going to get anything here, either. Everything I got is sunk into this place. The boy could have had this business given to him outright someday, but he always thought he was too good for dirty mechanic work," he added bitterly. "Instead, he holes up with his computer and spends all his money helping the women who marry him because they need someone to take care of them."

Furious now, Stevie drew herself up to her full five feet two inches, clenching her hands at her sides. "You might be my father-in-law, Mr. McKellar, but I've got to tell you… You're a—a…" A word Cole wryly used after frustrating business transactions popped into her head, and she applied it with no trace of humor. "A moron."

His brows lowered into a deep V of disbelief. "What did you—"

"I did not come here to ask you for money," she said, cutting him off. "And how dare you make that assumption?"

"Then why would you come here behind Cole's back?"

"Because I'm a moron, too," she replied with a bitter shake of her head. "I didn't come to ask for anything. I came to offer something. I stupidly thought I could charm you into making a new start with your son. It never even occurred to me that a kind, honorable, courteous man like Cole would come from a father who is so rude and…and just mean."

"Look, I—"

She swept on, her hands fluttering in agitation. "You're intentionally blind if you can't see what a fine man your son has turned out to be. He works very hard and he has gained a great deal of respect from people who recognize his intelligence and competence. You should be proud of what he's accomplished rather than trying to make him feel guilty because he didn't want to take over this business. He never thought he was too good for mechanic work. That's not the kind of man he is. He simply pursued the work that best suited him and that made him happy, which is what any parent should want for his child. And by the way, he obviously respects you more than you do him. He told me that you're a damned good mechanic, that there's not an engine in existence you can't tear down and rebuild, and that you've invested very wisely in your business and have been very successful with it."

"He said that?"

She was on a roll and in no mood to listen now. "He didn't tell you about the baby because he didn't think you'd care. I thought maybe he was wrong. I thought maybe you'd like the chance to be a granddad to this little boy. Despite the appalling example you've set, Cole will make a wonderful father. This child and I are very lucky to have him in our lives. You're the one who's losing out. So, here's the deal, Mr. McKellar. If you have even a lick of sense inside that stubborn head of yours, you'll apologize to your son and try to repair some of the damage your stubborn pride has done to your relationship."

She could tell by the stunned look in his dark eyes that gruff, stern Jim McKellar was not accustomed to being talked to in that manner. Did no one ever stand up to him when he acted like a total jackass? If not, it was past time someone did.

"I'm leaving," she said, moving to the door with as much dignity as she could manage in her condition. "I assume you have your son's telephone number if you come to your senses."

She didn't give him a chance to reply before she let herself out and stalked to her car.

Her seething resentment on Cole's behalf lasted until she'd arrived home. She stamped into the house that still smelled of fresh paint and sawdust. The staircase to the second floor was now completed, leading to a small landing that branched into a nearly completed office on either side. She thought she could work quite comfortably in hers and Cole had assured her he felt the same way about the one he'd helped design for himself. It wasn't like having an entire house to himself, of course, but it would be very nice, she assured herself in an attempt to assuage a sudden, inexplicable ripple of guilt.

That boy has always been a sucker for a woman in trouble.

He spends all his money helping the women who

marry him because they need someone to take care of them.

Jim's acrimonious comments echoed in her mind as she walked through the empty house.

As often as she tried to convince herself that Cole had gained as much from their marriage as she, there was always a niggling suspicion that he was giving the most. She'd wanted to believe his wants were simple—a compatible wife, a family, a nice home to return to from his business trips. But she was tormented by the feeling that there was something more he needed, even if he wasn't aware of it himself. She'd thought reconciling him with his father would be a gift she could give to him, but now she wondered if maybe she'd just made everything worse.

She groaned and pushed her hands through her hair. She only hoped Cole wouldn't someday regret the day he'd ever moved next door to her.

As Stevie had predicted, Cole was not thrilled when he found out what she'd done. Still, he seemed as annoyed with her for making the drive by herself as he was for interfering with his family.

"That was reckless," he said, his tone as critical as it had ever been with her. "What were you thinking?"

She shook her head impatiently. She'd understand if he was angry. She'd even been prepared for a flash of previously unseen temper, but not for this reason. "Obviously, I'm perfectly capable of making an hour's drive. I'm trying to apologize for butting into your affairs without checking with you first."

"It was a two-hour drive round trip," he reminded her. "And anything could have gone wrong. You don't need to be taking chances at this stage in your pregnancy."

Was he redirecting his irritation at her for speaking with his father into a less complicated and slightly more justifiable, in his mind at least, annoyance with her for risking her health?

"I drove carefully and, of course, I had my phone with me. It's not as if your father lives on a different continent, though you wouldn't know it from the way you two behave."

He drew a deep breath and she wondered if he was mentally counting to ten.

"Say what you need to say, Cole."

Another ten-count and he finally spoke, though he kept both the words and the tone coolly controlled. "I appreciate what you were trying to do, Stevie. You just wanted to help."

Taken by surprise, she frowned. "It's okay if you're mad. You can tell me. I know I stepped over the line."

He shrugged, his dark eyes revealing nothing. "Like I said, you were trying to help. You just didn't realize what you'd married into when it comes to your father-in-law."

She hadn't told him everything because she didn't want Cole to become too outraged on her behalf in case the two men mended their bridges in the future. She'd said only that his father hadn't seemed pleased by her visit, nor had he shown particular enthusiasm for a grandchild.

Cole didn't bother with further chastisements. He merely drew a long, deep breath and then said, "In the future, maybe it would be best if we discuss things like this first, though you hardly need my permission to do anything. Just be careful, okay?"

She blinked rapidly. Seriously? That was it? "I'm just saying, it's okay if you're angry. You don't have to walk on eggshells around me."

Squeezing the back of his neck, he looked at her with an expression that bewildered her. Was he actually amused now? "Honestly, Stevie, do you *want* me to be mad? I mean, if it's important to you, I'll try to work up some righteous indignation, but I'd rather have dinner, if it's all the same to you. That chili smells really good."

Of course she didn't want him to be mad, she fumed as she turned to finish preparing the meal. He was absolutely correct that she'd meant well, that she'd tried to reach out to his father for Cole's sake. She'd been fully prepared to make those arguments if he'd scolded her. So why did it perturb her that he'd made her case for her, instead?

She just wanted him to feel free to be himself with her, she thought with a sigh. She didn't want to be seen as a damsel in distress. She wanted him to know she was here for him, too, if ever he happened to be the one in distress.

Would calm, controlled, utterly self-sufficient Cole ever need anything from her? And if he did, would he ever have enough faith in her to show it?

A week later the home offices were ready for occupation. It had taken only five weeks from clearing the attic to the last touches of paint. Stevie was delighted to have the construction out of the way so they could move Cole's things over, finish the nursery and set up the guest room. Meanwhile they'd decided to sell his house, agreeing that what had been Stevie's home would now serve their needs well for many years to come.

They took a weekend off work to move boxes into the

new offices and unpack. Cole had taken advantage of her design experience to help him with his space. He'd told her what he liked and approved the plan she'd then created for him. She'd made use of artwork and other items from his house mixed with a few new pieces she'd bought, keeping the color palette warm and earthy. Her office, of course, was a mix of the grays and greens she loved with corkboard on the walls for the notes and photos and inspiration pages that she always seemed to collect.

Dusty insisted on "helping" with the office setup, winding around their ankles, rubbing her cheek against everything she could reach to make sure it was marked with her scent. Stevie petted the cat fondly, thinking this was as much her home now as it was theirs.

"Here?" Cole asked, holding a framed print of an antique map up against the wall opposite the dormer window.

Stevie tilted her head and studied it with narrowed eyes. "Just a little lower. There. Hang it right there."

He marked the spot with a pencil, then reached for a hammer and nail. Stevie arranged two small bronze figurines of samurai warriors on a shelf above his computer monitor, smiling at the whimsy of them. Cole had only a few personal treasures he cared to display, but he'd shown a fondness for this set, which he said had been a gift. He didn't elaborate and she didn't ask for details, but she took care in finding just the right spot to display them.

Satisfied, she opened another box while he hung the print. A framed photograph smiled up at her when she looked into the box. It rested on several other frames and what might have been a couple of photo albums and scrapbooks. "Oh, I'm sorry. This looks like personal rather than business stuff."

He glanced over his shoulder and went still. "I'm not planning to unpack that box."

She couldn't resist taking out the 5"×7" frame, gripping it carefully between her hands as she studied the woman in the photograph. She wasn't beautiful, not even pretty, exactly, but she had a sweet, pleasant face and a generous smile. Her hair and eyes were brown, her skin tone slightly olive. Though this was only a headshot, cropped just below the shoulders, Stevie got the impression she'd been very thin. The expression in her eyes spoke of warmth and kindness underlain with difficult experience, or maybe Stevie was just projecting what little she'd heard about her. "This is Natasha?"

"Yes."

"She looks amazing," she said sincerely.

"She was. You'd have liked her."

"I'm sure I would have."

Replacing the photo in the box, she closed the lid gently. Cole lifted it onto the top shelf in the big storage closet, then closed the shutter-style door.

Settling on the floor in front of his desk to start connecting wires, he glanced up at her as she stood there watching him. "You can ask," he said, either reading her expression or knowing her so well.

"Only a couple of questions," she promised.

He nodded.

"How did you meet her?"

"We met in high school. She was born with a heart condition and she was sick a lot. One of our teachers asked if I would tutor her in math to help her keep up. We became friends. Lord knows she needed a friend then."

"Why?"

He reached beneath the desk, his voice muffled when he said, "Bad family life. Alcoholic parents, couple of troublemaker brothers. My dad didn't like me hanging around her because he didn't approve of her family—not that anyone else did, either. Even outside of that, everyone treated her differently because they thought of her as sickly. Which I guess she was, but she had a sharp, creative mind and she was trapped in a family that didn't much value academic accomplishments."

Like his own father? Had that lack of parental bonding drawn Natasha and him together?

"Anyway," he continued, emerging with a surge protector cord in hand, "her health got better after high school and she was able to attend college on a full scholarship. Then one of her brothers went to jail and her dad got sick. Her mother tried to talk her into quitting college and moving home to serve as a live-in cook and maidservant, despite Tasha's own health issues. She refused and was forbidden to come home after that, even on holidays. She didn't mind too much since her family's idea of celebrating a holiday was drinking too much and getting into a brawl."

"How on earth did she turn out so well coming from that background?"

He shrugged. "We always joked about it being a recessive gene. She didn't think she was better than her family," he clarified, "but they led a life that didn't interest her, and they couldn't accept her for being different."

That statement seemed to Stevie to even more strongly reinforce her feeling that Cole and Natasha had connected over their similar family issues, though Cole had been spared the alcoholic parents and criminal brothers.

"Anyway, Natasha and I got married not long after college graduation. It seemed like the right move at the time for both of us."

"Your father didn't approve." That wasn't a guess, of course, since Jim had made it clear enough.

"No. Our relationship, which was already strained by my choice to study computer science rather than car mechanics, has been even more distant since. I entered grad school and Tasha got a desk job processing insurance claims. We had almost six years together. Her health was stable enough for the first few years that we were encouraged to start planning a future. We talked about maybe adopting a child—but then, five years ago, she caught pneumonia. She was never able to recover fully, and it was too much for her weak heart to take."

She searched his face. Though he wore no particular expression, his eyes looked dark and clouded. "I'm sorry," she whispered.

He nodded and plugged in another piece of equipment.

She leaned down to brush a light kiss against his cheek. "Thank you for sharing that with me. And now I should probably start dinner."

He pushed himself to his feet and brushed off his hands. "Why don't we go out tonight? We've been working so hard today there's no need for either of us to cook. How about Italian?"

"That sounds perfect. Just let me freshen up and I'll be ready to go."

Minutes later, when she smoothed her hair in front of her bathroom mirror, she saw how tired she looked. No doubt her sharp-eyed husband had noticed. He would feed her and bring her home and make sure she rested.

She had no doubt Cole was very fond of her. Why couldn't that be enough for her?

Her hand fell slowly to her side as the answer hit with a jolt. Despite all her resolutions against fairy tales and unrealistic expectations, her foolish heart had led her into trouble again. She'd fallen head over heels in love—perhaps really in love for the first time in her life—with a man who was fully deserving of her heart. And yet, still a man who couldn't give her what she'd always longed for.

Chapter Ten

The wedding for Tess and Scott was beautiful, the party afterward noisy and fun. Scott's six-year-old twin nieces served as flower girls. They dashed around the grounds of Scott's parents' lovely home after the ceremony, twirling in their pretty yellow dresses splashed with red poppies and tied with long red sashes. Tess's small family mingled easily with Scott's larger one, everyone looking happy to be there to celebrate.

There'd been quite a bit of teasing at the reception about Tess's two pregnant bridesmaids. Jenny was already almost as big as Stevie. Wearing floating knee-length dresses and carrying poppy bouquets, they'd smiled and perhaps sniffled a bit as their friend had exchanged vows with her love.

"You should sit down," Cole suggested as the warm June afternoon wore on. "You're starting to look a little strained."

Acknowledging the logic in his advice, she found a seat at one of the yellow-draped tables set up beneath a fluttering canopy. "I have a touch of a headache," she admitted in a low voice. "It's not bad, just a little annoying. I guess it's from the heat."

He frowned in concern. "Do you want to leave?"

"Not just yet." She looked around the milling, laughing crowd who seemed in no hurry to break up the party. Scott and Tess were obviously having just as much fun, neither of them looking impatient to cut their special event short. "Soon."

"Let me get you something cold to drink, then."

She smiled up at him. "Thank you, Cole."

"He's certainly attentive this afternoon," Jenny commented, sinking gratefully into a chair close to Stevie's.

Realizing she'd been rubbing her temple, Stevie dropped her hand and nodded. "Yes. Not quite to Gavin's levels of hovering, but I'd say I'm being well cared for."

Jenny laughed ruefully. "I made the mistake of mentioning last night that my back hurt a little and Gavin asked if we needed to call his EMT buddy to take me to the hospital. I swear, if he doesn't have a nervous breakdown before this baby gets here, it will be a miracle."

Stevie laughed. "It's probably only going to get worse after your daughter arrives. I can't stop giggling when I think about Gavin with a daughter."

Her hand resting affectionately on her swollen middle, Jenny made a face, though a smile lit her eyes. "He's been in a daze ever since we found out it's a girl. Our poor daughter is going to have a cop dad who'll scare off all the boys who even look at her. I'm sure I'll do my share of refereeing between them in about fourteen years, though something tells me Gavin and his daughter are going to adore each other despite the inevitable clashes."

"I have no doubt," Stevie agreed in amusement.

She glanced across the lawn toward the food tables, where Cole had been detained in a conversation with Gavin. Probably comparing notes on living with pregnant wives, she thought with a chuckle. Her gaze lingered on her husband's face. He seemed to enjoy the gathering of her friends, but she knew he'd be glad to get back home. He had a big work project underway and he would probably put in a few extra hours that evening. He would likely stay up a couple hours after she turned in, then he'd try not to disturb her as he slid into bed. She would rouse when he joined her, as she usually did, and would nestle against him in the cozy sleeping arrangement they'd settled into. She always slept better now when he was there, the room seeming empty and somehow darker when he was away.

"Are you still trying to pretend you don't absolutely adore your husband?" Jenny asked quietly, her gaze focused on Stevie's expression with the wisdom of more than two decades of friendship.

Stevie latched automatically onto a strand of hair, winding it slowly around one finger. "Cole is a very special man," she said after a moment.

"And you're in love with him."

She shrugged helplessly, feeling her eyes burn with a prickle of tears she refused to release. She could never deceive her oldest friend. "How could I not be?"

"And Cole?"

"Is very fond of me. *Very* fond of me," she emphasized. "We have a good life. We've had a great time getting the house ready for the baby and talking about the future. We were good friends for a year before we married, of course, and we've only gotten closer since."

She knew there was no call to justify her marriage to Jenny, but for some reason she wanted to emphasize her good fortune.

"You have seemed happy," Jenny conceded slowly, her brow creased with concern.

Stevie forced a smile. "I know how lucky I am. Really, Jen, don't worry about me. I couldn't ask for anything more."

What more could she expect, anyway? Passionate, flowery words? That would never be Cole's style. Guarantees that he would never desert her or this child? She was confident that would never happen. Promises that he would always be a loyal and faithful husband? Knowing this innately honorable man as well as she did, that was a given. Assurances that he appreciated her mind, her competence, her talents and her body? He made those things known in a myriad of ways every day, not always in words but certainly through action.

Which meant that she just needed to grow up and learn to be satisfied with what she had.

He and Gavin approached the table together. Cole handed Stevie her cold beverage, then rested a hand lightly on her shoulder as he asked her friend, "How are you holding up, Jenny?"

"I'm fine, thank you," she assured him, accepting a glass from Gavin. "I'm having a wonderful time."

"This time next year our babies will be babbling together when we sit around a table." Stevie smiled as she envisioned many pleasant future gatherings.

"Hmph," Gavin grumbled, though he was obviously suppressing a grin when he pointed a finger at them.

"I'm going to be keeping an eye on that boy of yours around our daughter."

"Just so that daughter of yours doesn't break our boy's heart," Cole shot back with a smile.

Stevie reached out to pat her husband's cheek as the others laughed. "Isn't he a cutie?"

Cole growled, but she could tell he didn't really mind her teasing. He was getting used to it by now.

Though large social gatherings with a lot of strangers weren't really his style, Cole had a good time at the wedding. It helped that it wasn't a stuffy, formal affair and that he already knew Stevie's closest friends. He enjoyed watching her with them. The bond between the three women was so strong it was almost visible. Their men fit in well enough, but that special friendship was the heart of the group, the glue that would hold them all together in the future.

He knew these people would be part of his life now, but he didn't mind. They had accepted him warmly despite the early doubts he'd sensed in Jenny and Tess. He believed he'd convinced them that he would never intentionally hurt their friend. His wife.

He'd sat in a folding chair among the rest of the audience as Tess and Scott exchanged their vows, though it had been hard for him to take his eyes off Stevie. She'd looked so pretty standing up there in her bridesmaid dress, her blond curls falling soft and loose to her shoulders, her big blue eyes luminous with emotion. Even round with pregnancy, she was beautiful. He was always proud—and a little amazed—to be seen with her.

He knew she would honor the vows they'd exchanged in their own wedding ceremony. Maybe he wasn't her

Prince Charming, but she seemed satisfied with a knight in practical armor.

Satisfied. For some reason, the word made him wince, though he couldn't quite explain why.

Just what would happen if Stevie's satisfaction ever waned, if she decided he wasn't what she wanted, after all? She was a woman of her word, but he'd never want to hold her to it if she truly longed to leave. Would he ever know for certain if her mother's restlessness nagged at her, too?

For only a moment as she chatted and laughed with her friends, he imagined how it would feel to go back to the life he'd had before they'd eloped. Just him and his cat alone in a comfortable, quiet house. He'd thought himself happy enough at the time, but now the vision made his chest muscles tighten painfully.

Impatient with himself for wasting even a minute of this nice afternoon with pointless imaginings, he shook off the odd mood and focused again on his determination to make sure Stevie had a good time. He couldn't even speculate about returning to a life without Stevie in it. Just thinking about it made his heart hurt—and this was neither the time nor place to analyze his convoluted feelings for his wife.

Two weeks before her due date, Stevie stood in the center of the sage-and-cream nursery, looking around in satisfaction. Everything was in place and waiting to welcome the baby, whose name was still to be determined. She had to admit she was the holdup in that respect. Cole had made several suggestions and had liked several of her recommendations, but she simply couldn't make up her mind on this momentous decision.

She smiled a little as she remembered how tactfully he'd vetoed a few of her more fanciful brainstorms.

"I'm not saying the kid would get beat up on the playground if you give him that name," he'd said about one of them, "but maybe we'd better start martial arts training early."

Laughing, she'd agreed with him that maybe it wasn't the best choice for an Arkansas boy, and had gone back to her research.

She rubbed her temple against another dull headache as she absently repositioned a striped-shade ceramic lamp on the antique nightstand she'd found in a dusty resale shop. The turtle night-light sat beside the lamp, smiling blandly up at her. The pretty little bassinet from Branson was displayed in the center of the room. Next to the new crib sat an overstuffed nursing chair and ottoman—a joint gift from Tess, Jenny and their spouses. It still brought a lump to her throat to admire it, and she knew she would think of her dear friends every time she rocked her baby there.

Straightening the soft hand-knit throw draped over the back of the chair, she thought about resting there for a few minutes now. Her head was really starting to hurt and her back ached. Maybe she needed a nap. Though it was a Saturday, she'd tried to work a little that morning upstairs in her office, and maybe she'd simply sat too long in an uncomfortable position. Not that there was any truly comfortable position these days.

"Stevie?" Cole strolled into the room with a package in his hands. He'd been outside on this hot, late July Saturday and his face was still a little flushed from the humid heat, his hair rumpled the way she liked it best.

Already in a sentimental mood, she felt her heart swell even more at the sight of him. She loved him so much. Lately she'd been thinking she should just tell him how she felt. She'd almost done so a time or two, but something had always held her back. Perhaps the fear of making him uncomfortable, of creating awkwardness between them as the baby's arrival grew ever closer. Maybe even the nagging fear that he would smile indulgently and pat her arm as if writing off her feelings to those annoying pregnancy hormones. It wasn't like her to be shy with her feelings, but in her current vulnerable state, she thought it might break her heart if he didn't believe her.

Unaware of her inner conflict, he said absently, "Looks like maybe another baby gift. The return address on this package says it's from a P. Rose."

"Pepper Rose," she said with a quick smile of delight. "The client I told you about."

"Oh, yeah. You did her kitchen a while ago, right? Big job up on River Ridge?"

"Yes, that's the one. She's such a sweetheart. It was nice of her to—Oh, God."

The pain ripped through her skull like a nail driven into her temple. She put both hands to her head, squeezing her eyes shut against a flash of light, fighting down a wave of nausea.

She heard a soft thud as the package hit the carpeted floor, and then Cole was beside her, his hands on her upper arms. "Stevie? What's wrong?"

"My head," she gasped just before her knees buckled.

He caught her—as she knew he always would.

The pain was overwhelming. "Cole?"

He gathered her close. "I'm here."

"Don't leave me."

"Never. Let's get you to the hospital."

* * *

Time passed in a haze of pain and fear. Stevie was rushed straight into an emergency exam room, her clothes stripped away, IVs and monitors quickly attached to her. She clung tightly to Cole's hand when he was allowed near her.

"I'm here, Stevie." His voice was hardly recognizable.

She gazed up at him through pain-clouded eyes. For the first time since she'd met him, she saw Cole's face raw with emotions—fear, compassion, helplessness. She thought his hand trembled around hers, though it was hard to distinguish her own unsteadiness from his.

"Tell the doctor…" She recoiled against another wave of pain, then forced out the words. "Tell them to save the baby."

"Stevie…"

"Mr. McKellar? You need to step out now," a nurse said, her voice kind but firm. "You can sit in the waiting room. We'll keep you updated."

His hand tightened on Stevie's as if he wanted nothing more than to refuse to leave her, but he nodded grimly and leaned over to press a gentle kiss on her lips. "You remember the bet we made at the mini golf course on our honeymoon?"

She forced an answer through another wave of pain. "I—I remember."

"I never collected on that bet," he reminded her, his tone intensely serious. "I'm naming the prize now. I want a Valentine dance with you at our golden wedding anniversary celebration. You got that, Stevie? You have to pay up, you promised."

A low moan escaped her despite her efforts to swallow it. She managed a nod and a whispered, "I promise."

"Mr. McKellar?"

Groaning in frustration, he straightened and released her hand. "I'm going. You take care of my wife, you hear? Whatever it takes, you save her."

"I love you, Cole," Stevie croaked but she didn't think he heard her. Didn't even know if he was still in the room. She closed her eyes and gave herself over to the medical personnel surrounding her.

She woke much later in a narrow hospital bed, still hooked to IVs and monitors but mercifully free of pain. She sensed the discomfort lurking just outside the range of the medicines controlling it, but for now she was okay, just still very sleepy. The overhead lights were dimmed and the hallways quiet outside the room, so she guessed it was nighttime, perhaps quite late. She vaguely remembered that she was in an ICU unit being closely watched by medical staff. For the moment, however, no one hovered over her bed, which was a relief.

Her restless hand fell on her noticeably flatter stomach and she gasped in sudden fear. The baby?

"He's fine. I have him."

Cole's reassuring voice came from close by. She turned her head to see him settled in a visitors' chair with a snugly wrapped bundle in his arms. An empty portable plastic bassinet sat beside him. He glanced back down with a ridiculously besotted—and absolutely heart-melting—expression on his face. "Looks like Mom's awake," he said softly.

Her heart tightened.

Cole stood and carried the baby to the bed, looking so big and strong in contrast. "He's doing great. The nurse will be back in a couple minutes to check on you both, but so far everything is good."

Her gaze focused without blinking on that little bundle, the beautiful little pink face topped with a blue knit cap. "He's—he's okay?"

"He's perfect. I don't know how much you remember, but he weighed six pounds, one ounce, and he's seventeen inches long. Little, but healthy. He's got quite a set of lungs on him. I heard him protesting an exam a little while ago. Both of you will be staying a few nights here, but everything looks good. Ready to hold him?"

"Oh, yes."

Smiling in response to her fervency, Cole shifted her loose hospital gown to uncover an expanse of skin on which to carefully lay the baby. Cheek to breast, the baby nuzzled instinctively but didn't awaken. Cole rested a hand on the little back. "He's worn out from that fit he threw, I guess."

Stevie could hardly speak. The feel of the warm, damp little face against her skin was incredible. Her heart was so full of love she could barely breathe. She felt a jerk of nerves as she cradled him against her, cupping his little head through the snug cap. He was so tiny. So fragile. So totally dependent.

Something made her look up at Cole then, and she heard the fierceness of her own voice when she said, "I could do this alone if I had to. I could take care of him and support him. My mom did it. Twice. Lots of single mothers do it every day. I could handle it."

He took a step back from the bed, looking almost as if she'd slapped him. He schooled his expression quickly. "I have no doubt you could handle it. Are you telling me that's what you want?"

Her eyes were so heavy, her thoughts clouded. "I just…needed you to know," she murmured, snuggling the warm, sleeping baby as she drifted on a cloud of exhaustion and medication.

"Get some rest, Stevie," Cole said quietly. "I'll be here to watch over you. For as long as you want me."

There was more she needed to say, but her mouth simply wouldn't form the words. She slept, knowing he would be there when she woke.

Cole had believed his inner barriers had been so heavily reinforced during his youth that words could never hurt him now. He'd thought he'd learned years ago to keep his emotions protected, never expecting too much so he wouldn't be disappointed by rejection.

He'd loved Natasha, but he realized now that even with her he'd always held back a small piece of his heart. He'd grieved when he'd lost her, but it hadn't destroyed him.

It had taken Stephanie Joan McLane to storm those old barriers and lay claim to every molecule inside him. He wasn't sure how. Wasn't certain when the walls had fallen. But the events of this day had left him emotionally battered and bleeding.

Seeing the faces of the medical staff who'd attended to Stevie upon arrival, he'd immediately understood the gravity of her situation. Unable to think clearly enough even to make phone calls to her friends, he'd been almost paralyzed with shock, finding it hard to believe he was facing this tragedy again. He'd been wracked with fear of losing the baby. Of losing Stevie. Even knowing now that she would recover, he felt his throat tighten painfully just at the memory of that nightmarish hour.

Though her blood pressure had been carefully monitored during her pregnancy, it had soared rapidly and unexpectedly today. Pregnancy-induced hypertension.

Had she not gotten medical assistance in time, it could have led to seizures, a possible stroke—or even worse, he thought with a hard swallow as he tried to remember everything her doctor had said. Now that the baby had been delivered, Stevie would be fine, though she would remain under watchful care for a few weeks. The doctor had added that future pregnancies were not ruled out, though even more precautions would have to be taken. He couldn't even begin to think that far ahead. Especially without knowing exactly what Stevie had meant when she'd informed him she could raise this child on her own.

His gaze moved from the woman sleeping in the bed to the swaddled child dozing in his arms, Rocking the baby afterward had brought him back to sanity. he'd felt his world slowly begin to right itself again. Maybe his eyes had been damp and his throat dry, but his heart had returned to a strong, steady beat. He'd told himself that everything was going to be all right.

And then Stevie had woken to tell him she didn't need him, after all. He'd always been aware of that, but he'd thought they'd become a well-oiled team, each with strengths to bring to the union. He'd thought she could overlook his flaws, his messed up family, his sometimes-obsessive commitment to his work, in return for the parenting partnership she'd thought she wanted.

He should have known better. He shouldn't have fooled himself that the bubbly, indomitable, fearless Stevie needed anyone, much less him. Maybe she was more like her mother than she had realized, too restless and free-spirited to be tied to anyone other than the child she would certainly adore. How idiotic had he been to think an impulsive elopement based on her uncertainties and his loneliness would last a lifetime?

He'd promised himself he wouldn't try to hold her if she wanted her freedom. He could go back to the way things had been before. But while his job, his routines, his home might eventually be the same again, there would always be something missing. As uncharacteristically maudlin as it sounded, he would always know that he'd left his broken heart in Stevie's small, capable hands.

He settled back in the ICU visitor chair to keep watch over his wife for the remainder of the night. He tried not to think about what might come with morning.

Though sore from her C-section and still easily tired, Stevie felt much better the next afternoon. After a few nerve-racking initial attempts, she and the baby were both finally getting the hang of breast-feeding. She'd texted photos of the baby to her mother, brother and friends, the latter of whom were giving her a couple of days to recover before descending on her, though she knew they were impatient to meet little Liam.

She'd been moved out of ICU and into a regular room, though she would have to remain in the hospital for a couple more nights. Flowers, balloons and stuffed animals from family and friends surrounded her, but she had eyes only for the rosy-cheeked infant sleeping in a plastic bassinet drawn up next to the cushioned chair in which she sat. She wanted to regain her strength quickly and she couldn't do that lying in bed.

Every time she heard footsteps in the hall, she perked up, thinking it might be Cole. She'd sent him home a few hours earlier to get some rest and feed the cat. He'd been so tired from sitting up with her all night that his unshaven face had been a little pale. She'd slept a lot after the delivery, but every time she'd been awakened to tend to the baby, Cole had been there keeping watch, sometimes holding Liam with such tenderness that her heart had melted. He'd said very little this morning. She'd figured that in addition to exhaustion, he was understandably overwhelmed with everything that had happened yesterday.

She smiled brightly when the door opened and Cole came in, a vase of cheery yellow roses in one hand, the bag of personal items she'd requested in his other. "They're beautiful," she said as he made a place for the roses among the other gifts.

Looking a little sheepish, he all but shuffled his feet. "I thought you might like them. You've gotten quite a few deliveries while I was gone, I see."

"Yes, I have. But your roses are the prettiest."

She thought he might smile at that. He didn't. In fact, he looked entirely too serious as he went to look down into the bassinet. "How's he doing?"

"He's perfect," she said with a happy sigh. "He had a good feeding half an hour ago, and he's been sleeping like an angel ever since."

"And you?"

"I'll be glad to get rid of this thing," she said, waving a hand to indicate the IV line still taped into her arm. "I'm uncomfortable, of course, but it's not too bad."

"You wouldn't complain even if it was."

She shrugged, still studying his face. "Cole? Are you okay? Did you get enough rest?"

He sat on the edge of the rumpled bed, facing her chair. "I'm fine."

He didn't look fine. She tried again to get him to smile. "I've finally decided on my choice for Liam's middle name."

They'd agreed on Liam for a first name, but the middle name had been more difficult for her. Cole had left the choice to her, saying he had no real preference other than the first name they both liked. She'd known since this morning exactly what name best suited her son. "I want his name to be Liam Douglas McKellar."

A muscle twitched in Cole's jaw. He turned his head, but not before she saw a flash of emotion cross his face. Was he touched that she wanted to name her son after him? Happy? Sad? What?

"You aren't saying much today," she said, her eyes fixed on his somber profile.

He pushed a hand through his already tousled hair. "Look, Stevie. I just want you to know that whatever you need, whatever Liam needs, I will always be here for you. You have my word on that. But—"

He paused to clear his husky throat.

But? She didn't like the sound of that.

Her throat closed and she felt her hands begin to shake. Was Cole... Surely he wasn't trying to tell her he'd changed his mind about being married to her! Had the reality of actually seeing the baby, the physical reminder of the huge responsibility involved in caring for this tiny, totally dependent person, made him reevaluate the promises he'd offered so impulsively? Or had he realized he didn't want to raise another man's baby, after all? She was pretty sure she could actually feel her heart breaking at the very thought.

"Cole?" she whispered. "What are you trying to tell me?"

He took a deep breath. "I know you don't need me to help you raise him. So, if you've decided you'd rather do it on your own, if you've come to the conclusion that you married too quickly and for the wrong reasons, I won't stand in your way. I'll always be your friend, no matter what. I just want you to be happy."

Her heart started to beat again, slowly, tentatively, as she deciphered what she thought, what she hoped, he meant. She vaguely remembered the fiercely assertive speech she'd made to him while floating on pain meds and shock. "You think I want out of our marriage?"

He pushed his hands down his thighs as if drying nervous palms. "I know you weren't thinking clearly yesterday, but you said—"

That fleeting glimpse of emotion gave her encouragement to break in. "You misunderstood my point, Cole. I'm sure I was babbling, so I might not have made a lot of sense, but I'd have hoped you'd gotten to understand me a little better than this."

He raised his eyes to meet hers. For the first time since she'd known him, she saw self-doubt there. He'd always seemed so quietly competent, so relaxed and assured. But now he looked…almost afraid, she realized with a twist of her heart.

"You said you didn't need me."

Had he really believed she would stay with him only if he made himself indispensable to her? "What I was trying to say was that I could get by without your help, if necessary. I have other options. Family and friends. A nice home and a good job."

He nodded grimly. "I know. But I thought—"

Stevie had always been willing to risk everything for anyone important to her—family, friends, boyfriends. Only with Cole had she tried to be cautious, to put her fear of being hurt above those all-or-nothing instincts. Now she realized how foolish she'd been. What she'd found with him was worth more to her than any relationship she'd ever had before. This was not the time to become shy about expressing her feelings.

She met his eyes squarely. "I'm not staying with you because I need to, Cole. As grateful as I am to you for everything you've done, everything you've promised, that isn't why I want to be with you. I married you because I care very deeply about you. Maybe I didn't even understand how much at the time. During these past six months, I've come to realize that you've always been more than a friend to me. Even when I thought you weren't interested, even when I tried to convince myself I wasn't falling in love with you, I was fighting a losing battle. I won't stay with you because I need to, Cole, but because I want to. If you want me, too, that is."

"I want you," he said almost before she finished her speech. He surged off the bed and leaned over her chair, his glittering dark eyes locked with hers. "And though I know you don't really need me, I need you. I need your laughter, your passion, the color and energy you bring into my life. I don't want to give that up. Not now, not ever. When the doctors told me how much trouble you were in when we arrived at the hospital yesterday, I nearly lost my mind. I couldn't handle the possibility of losing you." He swallowed hard before he asked, "Will you stay married to me? Please?"

She reached up an unsteady hand to cup his firm cheek. "Yes."

Not even bothering to blink away her tears, she gave him a watery smile. "I made a promise to you on Valentine's Day in front of Pastor Dave and Luanne. I knew even then it was for a lifetime. Besides, I owe you a dance, remember? I would never renege on a bet."

"Damn straight," he murmured as he swooped down to claim her lips.

He drew back after a thorough kiss that only left her wanting more. "I'm going to do my damnedest to make sure you're never sorry, Stevie."

She shook her head in fond exasperation. She heard a little catch in her throat as she replied. "You don't have to earn my love. You have it. And I'm confident you care about me, too," she added bravely.

It would be enough, she told herself. She would never have to doubt Cole's loyalty and affection.

"I do care about you, Stevie. But I am also completely, totally in love with you."

She felt her eyes go wide, her lips part in surprise. "You—you are? Since when?"

"Since approximately the day I met you," he answered. "I didn't think I was your type. Wasn't sure I had anything to offer…until I found an excuse to make my move." He gave her a glimmer of a smile. "And then you'll notice I didn't waste any time."

She blinked rapidly against an incipient flood of tears. The last thing she wanted right now was to embarrass him. "I wasn't sure you… I mean, I know you loved Natasha…"

Her voice trailed off uncertainly.

That cheek muscle twitched again, but he spoke evenly. "Natasha was a special woman. I loved her for her courage, for her determination, for her intelligence and grace. I grieved for her when she died, and I felt guilty as hell that I didn't see how critical she was those last few days, even though I know she deliberately hid her pain from me. Then I fell for you, and to be honest, the guilt came back for a while when I thought about what a great life I'd have with you and Liam. Maybe that kept me from showing you just how much you'd come to mean to me. I won't hold back anymore. I love you, Stevie."

"I love you, too." Her voice was thick, but she managed to contain the tears to a mere trickle. "And I'm glad you don't feel guilty now. I'm sure Natasha would have wanted you to be happy. To have a family who loves you and makes you happy."

"She would have," he agreed. "So...don't scare me again the way you did yesterday, okay? When I thought I was going to lose you, too—" Emotion choked his voice, bringing a fresh film of tears to her eyes.

"I'm not going anywhere. I'm so blessed to have you for my husband. And our baby," she added, stressing the *our*, "is the luckiest little boy in the world to have you for a daddy."

He kissed her again as their son gave a little purr of contentment in the bassinet.

Epilogue

The nursery was quiet, all the lights out except for the glowing turtle on the nightstand. Stevie and Cole stood side by side next to the crib, holding hands as they gazed down at the angelic six-week-old baby sleeping soundly on his back. The fuzzy little tiger Cole had purchased on their honeymoon in Branson sat on a nearby shelf next to the floppy-eared Easter bunny, both faithfully on guard against bumps in the night. Cole had given Liam the new Stripy the day he'd come home.

"I'm glad the baptism this afternoon went so well," Stevie murmured. "And that everyone we love managed to be there with us."

The church had been filled with friends and family. Stevie's mother had spent the past week in their guestroom getting to know her grandson. Tom had made the drive to join them today, and had then taken their mom to spend a few days in Tennessee with him before she flew back to Hawaii. Cole's mother and stepfather had traveled from Florida and were staying in a nearby hotel for a few days. Even Cole's favorite uncle Bob had made a rare trip to Arkansas from his Wyoming ranch, where he'd lived for the past twenty years.

But it was the couple who'd arrived at the last minute before the service started that had most startled Cole.

"I have to admit," he said now, "I nearly fell over in surprise when Dad and Peggy walked into that church. I didn't know you'd even sent them an invitation."

She smiled faintly. "I didn't want you to be hurt again if it didn't work out, but Peggy and I conspired to make it happen. She's as fed up with the rift between you and your dad as I am. She told me your father regretted it, too, but he's just been too bullheaded to admit it. Now he can use getting to know Liam as an excuse to spend time getting to know his son again."

"He and Mom were almost civil to each other." Cole shook his head in amazement. "That's near miraculous in itself."

"I think Peggy warned your father that I would be very displeased with him if he wasn't on his best behavior," Stevie said with a little giggle.

Cole's grin flashed white in the shadowy room. "I'd say you definitely got your bluff in on him. Dad looked like he was taking no chances of triggering your temper again."

"I think underneath that gruff, prickly exterior, he might be softening a bit with age. I saw him tickling Liam's cheek and looking very pleased to get a smile in reward."

Not that anyone could resist this beautiful baby's sweet smiles, she thought without even trying to be objective.

Growing serious for a moment, Cole rested a hand on her shoulder. "Don't get too carried away, Stevie. Though I'll do my best to keep the goodwill going, I doubt the relationship between my dad and me will ever be warm and fuzzy."

She nodded. "Just as long as there is a relationship. Family is important. I want Liam to grow up surrounded by people who love him."

He wrapped his arm around her shoulders, murmuring, "There is definitely love in the home we've made for him here. He'll never have to doubt that."

"Yes, there is." She tugged his head down for a long, slow kiss to demonstrate just how much she loved and appreciated him.

Cole took a step backward and held out a hand to her. "Now that we've gotten the all clear from your doctor, I'm looking forward to showing you exactly how much I love you."

Confident that her romantic heart was finally safe in the place where it belonged, Stevie followed him with eager anticipation.

* * * * *

Don't miss out on the previous books in
Gina Wilkins' PROPOSALS & PROMISES *miniseries*
for Harlequin Special Edition!
A REUNION AND A RING and
THE BOSS'S MARRIAGE PLAN.
Available now wherever
Harlequin books and ebooks are sold.

"I'm so proud of the woman you've become." He trailed
his fingers along her upper arm, setting off a rush of
tingles that nearly unraveled her at the seams.

What was going on? Why had he touched her like
that? Did she dare read something into it?

The emotion glowing in his eyes warmed her heart in
such an unexpected way that she forgot her momentary
concern and pretended, just for a moment, that something
romantic was brewing between them.

She tossed him a playful grin. "I'm glad to hear you
say that, especially when you once thought of me as a
pest."

"Yeah, well, I wish I'd known then who the woman
that little girl was going to grow up to be. Things might
have been..."

His words drifted off, but her heart soared at the

mplication. Their gazes locked until he pulled his hand away and muttered, "Dammit."

"What's the matter?" she asked, although she feared what he might say.

"This is a real struggle for me, Sasha."

She had a wild thought that he actually might be attracted to her and waited to hear him out, bracing herself for disappointment.

He merely studied her as if she ought to know just what he was talking about. But she'd be darned if she'd read something nonexistent into it.

Graham raked his fingers through his hair. "I'm feeling things for you that I have no right to feel," he admitted.

"Seriously?"

"I'm afraid so. And I'm sorry, especially since you still belong to another man."

Sasha hadn't "belonged" to anyone in a long time, and if truth be told, the only man she wanted to belong to was Graham.

Don't miss
WED BY FORTUNE
by USA TODAY *bestselling author Judy Duarte,*
available June 2016 wherever
Harlequin® *Special Edition books and ebooks are sold.*

www.Harlequin.com

HARLEQUIN®

A *Romance* FOR EVERY MOOD™

JUST CAN'T GET ENOUGH?

Join our social communities
and talk to us online.

You will have access to the latest
news on upcoming titles and special
promotions, but most importantly,
you can talk to other fans about your
favorite Harlequin reads.

Harlequin.com/Community

 Facebook.com/HarlequinBooks

Twitter.com/HarlequinBooks

Pinterest.com/HarlequinBooks